Thirty and single? Well, getcha ass to the Gathering! Wait… what?

Lorelei is a hint over thirty—nobody better ask how much of a hint—and isn't sure why the hell she's been magically hauled to the land of werewolves. But she has. Which sucks. At least they stole her while she was at the gun range. Go Pink Pistol of Doom! So, they stole her, she stole a cell phone in return, and all is crazy in her new werewolf-laced world. It gets even crazier when, 1—she discovers her sisters have been kidnapped, too, and 2—werewolves are sexy as all get out. Lorelei is determined to come to her sisters' rescue and well, see what Dylan and Zeke have to offer.

Dylan and Zeke can't believe they've found their mate. Even though word was passed around that Wardens can have mates, they never thought they'd find theirs. And yet, here she is. Lorelei—gorgeous, lush, and curved in all the right places—calls to their magic and heats up their wolves. They want to lick her from head to toe… together. And they will, once they get that little gun out of her hands. Hell, maybe she could keep it. She is sexy even when she threatens their lives.

They found her and now they're gonna mate her… as soon as they take care of the powerful five families threatening to take Lorelei from them. Blood may be involved. Sucks to be those guys.

# Chapter One

Blog post by Ruling Alpha Mate Scarlet Wickham on July 22, 7:38 a.m....

*Day Two!*

It's day two of the annual Gathering, and the Ruling Alphas and the best Alpha Mate known to furry-dom are... exhausted.

We've got good news and bad news.

Good news is quite a few furballs found their mates! That includes one of my long lost cousins, Rebecca Twynham.

Bad news is Rebecca is one of my three cousins at the Gathering. That means there are still two other crazy chicks wandering the halls. Please be careful and approach them with caution. There is no telling whether they will be wearing their normal crazy coats or if being unknowingly teleported to the Gathering has given them new crazy clothing. When they shoot and/or attack you, it's because they don't know what you are... or they could know and shoot you anyway.*

Have a wonderful weekend and may you all find your mates!
*Scarlet Wickham*
Ruling Alpha Mate and HBIC**

*Disclaimer: Activities associated with the Gathering can, at times, involve substantial risk of injury, property damage, and other dangers. Dangers particular to such activities include, but are not limited to: hypothermia, drowning, broken bones, strains, sprains, bruises, concussion, heart attack, heat exhaustion, cuts, abrasions, burns, electrical shock, poisoning, and blunt trauma. By participating in and attending the Gathering, you agree not to hold the Gathering organizers or other attendants liable for such damage. You break it, but we still ain't buying it.

**HBIC: Head Bitch In Charge

~~≈~~

Blog post by Ruling Alpha Mate Scarlet Wickham on July 22, 7:56 a.m....

*Day Two Part Two!*

Really, people? Really? You can't just listen, can you? Did no one read yesterday's blog post?

To reiterate: Warden Born are at the Gathering for Warden Pairs. Alpha Marked are here for Alpha Pairs. Whether she's Warden Born or Alpha Marked, the women are protected by the same laws. And it really shouldn't take more than a sniff to figure out if she belongs to you. Werewolf speed dating does not require an overnight stay in your hotel room.

I promise. I order it, even.

Also, Lorelei Twynham was spotted near the Fire Hydrant Ballroom. Please keep your eyes peeled. There is a reward for her safe return. And by safe, I mean no bruises, bumps, or mating bite marks. So help you if you've taken your fangs to her.*

Have a wonderful weekend and may you all find your mates!
*Scarlet Wickham*
Ruling Alpha Mate and HBIC**

*Disclaimer: Activities associated with the Gathering can at times involve lotsa bad stuff and yada yada and all that crap.

**HBIC: Head Bitch In Charge, don't forget it.

~~≈~~

Text message sent by Ruling Alpha Mate Scarlet Wickham on July 22, 8:10 a.m....

You people exhaust me and I can't find my laptop. Quit being stupid, and if you get bashed in the head with a chair, it's your own damn fault. Lorelei and Paisley are my cousins. That automatically puts them in the batshit crazy dangerous category. Do not view their level of crazy as a challenge to subdue them. YOLO should not be applied to this situation. Yes, you only live once, but if they kill you I will bring you back from the dead and kill you again. Slowly. Now, if you feel the urge to approach and apprehend, find a real grownup and then order a kid's meal at the restaurant. No more steak for you! Bad doggie!

~~≈~~

Text message sent by Ruling Alpha Mate Scarlet Wickham on July 22, 8:11 a.m.…

P.S. If one of them kicks your ass, I am so taking pictures and posting them on Wereweb.com. You people annoy me.

~~≈~~

*Reply* text from Ruling Alpha Madden Harris on July 22, 8:12 a.m.…

Fucker. Get here. She's eating an éclair and we're gonna start without you.

~~≈~~

Text message sent by Ruling Alpha Mate Scarlet Wickham on July 22, 8:12 a.m.…

Please ignore Madden's text. God knows I love him, but the "new" button and "reply" button are too close together.

# Chapter Two

Anyone who said sleeping behind a potted palm tree was uncomfortable was… right.

Ugh.

Lorelei twisted and wiggled as much as she could, trying to find a comfortable position. Then she squirmed the other way and sighed when her back cracked. There, that made things a little better. She leaned back, resting against the wall, and once again silently thanked the hotel's interior decorator for giving her the perfect hiding place.

Twenty-four hours into this psychedelic run from hell and she was ready to call it a day already. Except, the more she watched two-legged people turn into four-legged wolves, the more she realized this whole episode might not be a psychotic break. It could, in fact, be a little bit real. A teeny tiny bit and she'd only admit that to people who were *not* holding white coats that had all of those scary straps and buckles.

But she wasn't ready to fully accept the fact that werewolves were real.

Real.

Holy fuck real.

And hot. But she wasn't addressing that, or thinking it, or even pondering how every man she'd spied was all hot and sexy from head to toe. *Hot* bared repeating.

Right. Not addressing because she had other things to think about. Such as how long could she remain undetected? Or, how could she get off the grounds, figure out where the hell she was, and get home?

She'd also really, really love a cup of coffee. Undetected-ly.

Lorelei's stomach grumbled, reminding her she hadn't eaten in a while. Nice. Add low blood sugar to her ball of fucked-upped-ness.

She also figured since she was having a little pity party, she'd take a sec to whine about her whining.

Lorelei took a deep breath and fought for calm. She had allowed herself to panic for the first hour—or several—yesterday and it was time to get her poop in a group and focus.

Since she was awake at the butt crack of whatever o'clock, she figured she could figure out what was on the agenda for the day by turning on the cell phone she'd stolen. She'd feel bad about being a thief later. Or never.

She shifted and shimmied until she no longer slouched. She sat cross legged behind the tree, the massive pot keeping her hidden. A quick glance showed no one had stirred, and she was still alone in the hallway. It spanned a good thirty feet wide, the floor covered with large marble tiles. They shined in the dim light, creating an ethereal glow. She knew it'd sparkle as the sun rose, but this shine was calming.

Well, calming-ish.

She was still on the run.

From werewolves.

The good news was the tiles would announce anyone coming. There was no way to *not* be heard walking over the hard surface.

Lorelei raised her head higher, taking another quick look before she settled in. The gun she'd been holding when she was snatched rested on the floor beside her, the glaring pink contrasting with the beige marble. Her only saving grace was the weird black hole thing that transported here had appeared while she was at the gun range. Of course, she'd also been instructing a class on safety procedures, and she had no idea what they'd seen. She wondered if they'd rallied a search team or if what'd happened was somehow masked.

*FYI, Lorelei, you're not gonna think about the black hole thing or what created it or even how it was created.*

She was losing it. She was now talking to herself. *Nice.*

One second she was pointing out her little .22's safety and the next she was standing on a roof, wind whipping her hair and the rush of air cutting off any other sounds.

Poof.

Not long after that she discovered werewolves were real. And they didn't seem too concerned with a woman emerging from the rooftop stairwell.

They obviously weren't big on security.

Lorelei felt her panic rising and rushing forward, reminding her she'd been magically dragged to a hotel in God knew where and she was alone with a bright pink gun and a stolen cell phone.

The pink had seemed like a good idea at the time. Now that she had to be circumspect, she realized black would have been a better choice. Or even purple. The eggplant would have blended in better than *neon* pink.

She was letting her mind wander again. Dammit.

She shook her head and focused on the smartphone. She held down the button at the top and waited for the manufacturer's logo to appear. It wasn't long before the device was asking her for a password, and it took even less time to gain access.

The phone's owner had practically asked for the thing to be stolen when he left it on the windowsill. And *then* he made the password 1234? Seriously?

He should have just offered it to her on a silver platter.

The cell phone was still on silent, not making a sound as it displayed the home screen. Small numbers appeared by each icon, signaling that the previous owner had several emails and texts.

Lorelei only felt a tiny bit guilty reading them. Tiny bit. Considering the hot guy was probably a werewolf, her guilt took a mini-vacay.

When the numbers quit increasing, she began with texts.

Someone named HBIC kept texting the guy…

*Dangerous…*

*Idiot…*

*Dumbass furballs…*

Whoever the hell it was, he or she obviously knew about the wolf stuff going down. She was actually smiling the closer she got to the most recent messages and that was about the time her heart did this whole stopping thing.

Because…

*You managed to follow a few directions. *high five* Now, find Lorelei and Paisley Twynham and I shall be one happy Head Bitch. If you do not turn them over carefully and perfectly unharmed, I will In Charge your ass. Mwah! SW.*

Lorelei read the message again. And again. And again for the third time.

Yeah, someone knew she was here. Here and they wanted her *and* Paisley.

She switched to the phone's email system and discovered other messages that left her blood running cold. At least one blog post mentioned Rebecca and the fact that her youngest sister found her "mates."

It was some weird magic-wielding werewolf cult. It had to be. And they, for some reason, decided the Twynham sisters were the perfect kidnapping targets.

"Oh fuck," she whispered, stunned at seeing the words in black and white. Her stomach lurched, and it threatened to empty its non-existent contents all over the pristine marble. "Oh fuck, oh fuck, oh fuck…"

"That sounds like a wonderful idea." The deep voice stroked its way down her spine, sending sizzles of arousal over her nerves. Her whole body pulsed with sudden need. That throb came again and a soft light filled the tight area before it retreated and she gasped with the sensation.

Gasped because she'd never been so desperate for a guy *and* because when she raised her gaze, she found herself staring into a set of sparkling green eyes.

Then, because she was a little bit crazy and a lot scared, she did what any other red-blooded chick with a gun—and latent rage from being physically assaulted two years ago—would do. And by latent she meant burning like a thousand suns. She'd never be caught unable to defend herself. She hadn't spent countless hours learning self-defense and twice as long at a gun range for no reason.

Lorelei pointed that gun right at Mr. Green Eyes.

More like right *between* those pretty green eyes.

*

Zeke's first reaction when the barrel of the gun touched his forehead wasn't an attempt to disarm the woman or thoughts of how to get free without getting shot. With the cold muzzle pressed against his skin, bullet chambered and threatening to tear through his brain, he didn't duck or snatch it from her.

He snorted.

The stranger narrowed her hazel eyes, the mixture of greens and browns encouraging him to take a deeper look. She placed her thumb on the hammer, slowly easing it back until a familiar click reached his ears. Just as gradually, she released it and wrapped her thumb around the butt once again. She quirked a single dark brow, the delicate line rising in a graceful arch.

Since it wasn't like he could leave without getting shot, he remained still and took his time looking the woman over. He noted the delicate slope of her nose along with its pert tip. Her lips were lush and plump, begging for a kiss, the color reminding him of fresh strawberries at the height of summer. He followed the line of her pale neck down to the hint of her rounded breasts exposed by her polo shirt. The fabric stretched taut across her chest and he imagined them filling his palms.

Yes, she was one curvaceous package that he'd like to unwrap—when she wasn't pointing a gun at his head.

Though, his cock didn't seem to mind he was in imminent danger.

Come to think of it, neither did his wolf. In fact… his beast rumbled in approval of the female, encouraging him to get closer to her. The rapid thump of her heartbeat assaulted his ears and he sensed her fear and unease. He drew in another lungful of her scent, pulling it into him and savoring the sweetness.

His dick hardened fully, pressing against his jeans, and he nearly whimpered with the pleasure and pain.

He wanted her. Needed her. Had. To. Have. Her.

She trembled. From fear? From desire?

Another wave of her flavors hit him and he realized… it was both.

She drew in a deep breath and when she exhaled… When she exhaled, he realized why he wanted her so damned much and why he couldn't get enough of her aroma.

Because… not only did air escape her, she also released a tiny tendril of magic. It wasn't a lot, not a full push of her hidden power, but her skin took on a luminescent glow. A glow that encompassed her from head to toe and the familiar snaking symbols that covered her had him aching to stroke her.

A Mark.

Not an Alpha Mark, not a single entwined design that labeled her as a human female meant to mate a pair of alpha wolves. No, she was Warden Born, a human woman destined to mate with a Warden Pair.

Coincidentally, those lovely symbols didn't appear until she came near her mates.

Zeke drew in the surrounding scents, hunting for others in the vicinity. His wolf added its own abilities to the mix, determined to discover if she truly belonged to them. Already it felt possessive and was resolved to keep her from anyone other than himself and his partner, Dylan.

*Mine.*

No. *Ours.*

He hadn't had high hopes for the annual Gathering. It was the first time Warden Pairs were encouraged to meet the summoned females, after all. But now…

Now, the woman before him tilted her head to the side, eyes sparkling with anger, fear, and panic. But when she spoke her voice was smooth and unwavering. "You are going to slowly back away from the palm tree."

The words made him want to kiss her.

Damn, a feisty woman made his dick hard.

Instead of doing as she asked, he began his own interrogation.

"What's your name?" he murmured.

"Back the hell up. What's yours?" Her eyebrows lowered, eyes promising a whole lotta pain if he didn't listen to her.

He was never good at listening.

"Zeke Roberts." He traced the line of the gun's barrel with his gaze. "And based on your violent tendencies, I'm guessing you don't know why you're here."

"You haven't seen violence," she snapped back, her hints of fear replaced by red hot anger.

Her body glowed brighter with the new emotion, the strength forcing her magic forward.

"Yeah, B," he agreed with her even if it was a lie. Werewolves weren't exactly gentle creatures. At the moment, he imagined his little mate *had* experienced her own rounds of brutality. "You're probably right."

"B?"

"I could call you Back the Hell Up, but it's a mouthful." He grinned, just a small teasing smirk. Even if his heart rate was picking up the longer she held that pink monstrosity to his forehead, he had to pretend he was unconcerned. "So until you tell me your name, it's B or Beautiful. Your choice."

It was her turn to snort and it was wrong that the sound got him hotter.

"It doesn't matter. Step back and then you're gonna tell me how to get the hell out of here."

He wasn't gonna tell her anything, but he didn't say that. At least, not yet.

A soft buzz reached him, and the sound had him hunting the source. He glanced down and noted she clutched a cell phone in her free hand. A cell phone that was very familiar and had been missing since yesterday. A cell phone he'd been tracking via an app on his Warden partner's phone. At least it'd made its way into good hands.

And if she'd been reading the messages from Scarlet, their Ruling Alpha Mate… he internally winced. Internally, because he was sure if he suddenly moved he'd be one dead Warden.

The buzz on his stolen phone was echoed by his partner's phone clutched in his right hand. On its heels came another. And then a third.

He wondered if one of their Ruling Alphas got "new" and "reply" mixed up again.

Her aim steady, she raised the phone and stroked her thumb over the screen. It took no time for her to bring up the newest messages. Her eyes traveled over the words, sliding from side to side, and he wondered what their HBIC had to say now.

"Wanna read it aloud for the rest of the class?" He kept his voice low and easy.

"You know about this stuff, right?" Her voice trembled and his wolf snarled at him over her fear. As if he could hold her or soothe her when the woman was threatening his life.

Damned beast had some high expectations.

"What stuff?" he returned. Best to play dumb until he could figure out exactly what she knew… and didn't.

"This HBIC person. Werewolves or shifters or whatever. This hotel. All of it. You know about it. I'm not crazy, right?" The wavering of her words made him ache to hold her close. Her terror was practically a physical thing, punching him in the gut and shoving the air from his lungs.

"You're not crazy," he murmured. "And I'd be happy to explain everything if you come out of there."

Explain things and more. He was excited about the more. Not that he'd push their mating on her. If anything, Dylan would want to postpone sealing their bond for years if that's what she needed. Zeke was voting for an hour. Two at the most.

"I don't need explanations. I need to be gone." She swallowed hard, her throat rippling with the move. He wanted to lick her there, lick her and then let his mouth slide to her shoulder and… "I want out, but first you're gonna help me find Rebecca and Paisley." Her grip on the weapon tightened. "Get them for me and no one gets hurt."

*Shit.*

"Not Lorelei? If you've been reading the texts and emails, you know it's a set of three sisters." He had a sinking feeling he knew the answer to his question already, but he'd like his suspicions confirmed before he fucked himself over. Was he looking at Lorelei Twynham?

Her eyes widened, the color brightening due to her magic a bare moment before it settled back to its natural hue. "That's not necessary."

"Because you're Lorelei Twynham."

"I don't know what you're talking about," she snapped back and the words stung his skin. They cut into his flesh, and he swallowed the groan that came with the pain.

Damn, their little mate was fierce, her magic strong and unforgiving when she was annoyed. Zeke swore his dick was gonna break through his jeans.

"Alright. If that's the way you wanna play it." He drew a deep breath, tasting her flavors once again before he allowed himself to speak and fuck up his and Dylan's lives for a little while. A long while if they ended up dragged before the Ruling Alphas.

He just prayed the mate bond would alleviate some of her anger when all was said and done.

"I'm gonna move back real slow and you're gonna come out. I'll get you to Rebecca." *Eventually.* "They're still looking for Paisley and," he smirked, "Lorelei."

"Why are you people looking for us? Them. I mean, why are you people looking for *them*?"

Zeke figured some honesty was called for. "They're cousins to our Ruling Alpha Mate." He flicked his gaze to the cell phone and back to her. "The HBIC. She thinks she's funny." He shrugged. "Most the time she's pretty hilarious."

"We don't… They don't have any werewolf cousins. I'm pretty sure it's something *they'd* know."

"Considering the only ones who could mate a pair of wolves are human, I'm thinking *they* would have cousins who are human and Alpha Marked, and didn't realize it." She still gave him a skeptical glare, so he returned them to his initial idea. "It doesn't matter because you're going to come out of there and I'll get you to Rebecca."

"I want to leave."

"I understand." He still wasn't gonna listen.

"With my sis— With Rebecca and Paisley."

"I know. C'mon out. I'm not happy about you pointing a gun at me, but if anyone else sees, they'll be a lot more than unhappy." And then he'd have to kill everyone who growled at her.

That'd really piss off the Ruling Alphas. He wondered if the fact that he was protecting his mate—who also happened to be the Ruling Alpha Mate's cousin—mattered.

He figured it'd depend on how many he had to kill.

Lorelei—even if she wouldn't give him her name—pulled the gun from his head. "Step back."

He did as she ordered, not worried that she'd bolt. He stood not three feet from her and she'd have to get past him to flee. And really, other than a direct hit to the heart or head, a gunshot would annoy him more than hurt him.

When she emerged, he got another good look at their mate. Damn, she was a lot like Rebecca Twynham, yet so different. She was a tiny thing, generous curves in all the right places and despite her short size, she had enough attitude to make her seem six feet tall.

A nice, explosive package. Just what a strong Warden Pair needed.

He eased farther away, giving her more space as he gestured toward the nearby bank of elevators. "We'll head to the tenth floor."

Zeke didn't mention that Rebecca was on the eighteenth.

Or that he and Dylan were on the tenth.

*

Dylan Clarke towel dried his hair, running the terrycloth over his soaked strands. Even the heated shower hadn't soothed the tension in his body. He rolled his head, easing it from side to side as he fought to banish the unease that slithered through him.

Something was different. Not right or wrong, but… different.

His body pulsed with some unfamiliar need, and he dropped the towel to the ground, freeing his hands so he could stretch his arms over his head. Something was building inside him, extending its unseen claws into his flesh.

His wolf howled and wagged its tail in excitement. Okay, so it only freaked out his human half. The beast was happy as hell over what lingered in the air.

Dylan wished he could feel the same.

He shook his head. Sometimes his animal wasn't the brightest crayon in the box. It growled at him, reminding him that Dylan's human half had the brains, but his inner beast had the brawn.

Not that he wasn't a strong male in his own right, but the wolf… Between his wolf and Warden magic, there was a reason everyone kept their distance.

Everyone… Another shake of his head, dispelling the pang in his heart. It wasn't just wolves that stayed away from their Warden Pair, it was the female Warden Born at the Gathering as well.

He sighed. He wasn't sure why he was surprised. Maybe the five families were correct, maybe Wardens weren't truly meant to mate with human females. He hated to admit the crazed old fools had a point.

His wolf growled and snarled at him, anxious to tear into his flesh and rip those idiotic thoughts from his head.

*Yeah, yeah.*

He snared the towel from the ground and ran it over his chest once more. He had to get his shit together before Zeke returned. They were scheduled to attend the day's first round of Tests of Proximity.

The Ruling Alpha Mate had been correct when she'd described the event as werewolf speed dating. *Sit, sniff, next!*

It'd be a little different because they were Wardens. It was more like sit, glow in the dark, let's mate.

Dylan stared at his hand, wondering if his skin would pulse and glow like the Ruling Wardens'. When Emmett and Levy were with their mate, Whitney, they all adopted an ethereal light that surrounded the trio. That was also when Whitney's marks throbbed with her magic.

It was… the most beautiful thing he'd ever seen.

How could that be wrong? He shook his head. He couldn't believe it and yet…

The power that threesome wielded was deadly and dangerous, and Whitney was the most frightening of all. That female got a little pissy and… Dylan shuddered.

He was still torn on the issue. The five families had sacrificed so many to hide all evidence of the Warden Born, but he couldn't imagine Whitney Wickham was a mistake. That she hadn't been created with a purpose.

He sighed and padded toward the dresser. Zeke should be back with his phone soon and then they could get going. He still didn't understand how his partner lost his cell phone.

Wait. He did. Zeke was Zeke.

Dylan chuckled and drew out a pair of socks and boxers. It took no time to tug those on before he headed to the closet for his pressed slacks and button down shirt. He knew his friend would "rock out" with his chucks and ripped jeans.

He laid his clothing for the day on the king sized bed, fighting to ignore the tacky floral pattern and the way it clashed with his clothes. They needed to get a new decorator. Hotel Garou was home to the annual Gathering as well as a prime vacation spot for werewolves. It should look better than this.

He snared the slacks and slid them on, the tailored fit hugging his body in the right places while giving him room to move in others. Perfect. Considering what he'd paid for them, they damned well better be.

The beep and scrape of metal on metal announced that Zeke had returned. Dylan glanced at the clock and noted the time. His friend had just enough time to swap his crappy flip-flops for his equally crappy chucks and then they'd be on their way.

The low, deep murmur of Zeke's voice reached him, but he ignored it. The man was probably talking to himself. Again.

"C'mon, Z. We don't have much time left." Dylan raised his voice. He snatched his shirt from the bed and slipped his arms into the sleeves. Padding toward the bedroom's double doors, he called out again. "We gotta meet with—"

Dylan sucked in a harsh breath, the wind suddenly leaving his lungs and stealing his oxygen. He trembled, shaking from head to toe, and he reached for the wall to steady himself. With the sudden weakness also came a fierce rush of arousal. His cock went from soft to rock hard in an instant and he winced, realizing the tailor hadn't quite given him enough room *there*.

He fought for air, demanding his lungs respond. His wolf howled in his head, voicing its… joy? What the fuck? He couldn't spare a thought for the damned beast, not when his body throbbed with need and…

A gentle glow caught his attention, one that seemed to come from *inside* him. It pulsed in time with the beat of his heart.

Holy shit.

Holy shit.

She-she-she… *she* was near.

His female.

The hoarse murmurs from his partner reached him.

Their female.

Their female was near.

"Zeke," he pushed the single word past his dry lips. He couldn't do much more than that. Not when his cock was demanding attention while his wolf and heart ordered him to hunt her.

When his friend didn't appear, he forced himself into motion. He shoved away from the wall and shuffled forward. He gripped the door frame and leaned against it for support before he inched into the main room of their suite. The farther he delved, the brighter he glowed, his skin taking on a golden, ethereal hue.

"D, man, you gotta get your shit together." Zeke's words reached him a brief moment before large, rough hands grabbed him.

The touch of the other wolf settled him and took the harsh edge off whatever the fuck was going on.

He clutched Zeke's hand, taking strength from the male, and the connection gave him the power to stand upright and push away from the door. It also gave him the ability to catch the slightest movement to his right.

The movement of a single female.

A female glowing with the familiar mark of a woman who was Warden Born.

"Mine," he growled low. When she paled and her magic flared, his wolf growled at *him.*

"Ours," Zeke murmured, and Dylan jerked his head in a quick nod.

Theirs.

They'd strip her, fuck her, and then claim her.

She was theirs. Theirs with… a bright pink gun pointed at him.

Dylan rethought his plan.

*Disarm* her, strip her, fuck her, and then claim her.

# Chapter Three

Oh. Hell. No.

"I am all about being my own person, thankyouverymuch." Muzzle pointed at the floor, she kept her grip firm, index finger solid against the side of the weapon's barrel. She didn't want to shoot them before they told her what she wanted to know. Lorelei jerked her chin toward the half-naked hotness. "Last time I checked, Rebecca wasn't a guy who didn't know how to button his shirt."

Not that she wanted him to button his shirt. While Zeke was sexy-scruffy, this man was sexy-sophisticated. With his perfectly pressed slacks and crisp white shirt, he looked more like a businessman than a… werewolf. His chest certainly didn't look furry. No, there was a sprinkling of dark brown chest hair, but she also noticed his rippling abs. Another thing she noticed was that her mouth watered at the thought of tracing them with her tongue.

*That* thought had a shiver overtaking her, arousal like she'd never known assaulting her nerves. Damn, Zeke got her engines rumbling, but add in Hot Guy and she was ready to burst into flames.

She took a deep breath, fighting to calm the overwhelming need that hit her square in the gut. Or, a few inches lower and decidedly squishy at the moment. And twitchy. Because, only God knew how, her clit twitched with every sound that came from Zeke and Hot Guy. Especially when they growled together, their eyes slowly changing color until her hazel gaze was met by their yellowed orbs.

Yeah, okay, if she hadn't believed in the whole werewolf thing, that right there turned her into a believer. The new rush of fear also nearly bowled her over, sending a panic-laced tremor through her.

Lorelei met Zeke's gaze. "You told me you'd take me to Rebecca and since I'm not seeing her or Paisley, I'm thinking it's time to get back on the elevator and you can fulfill your promise."

The second man, werewolf, whatever, turned his attention to Zeke as well. The stranger took a step back and she pretended not to notice how her body reacted to him. She particularly ignored how her nipples pebbled. "Is she talking about Rebecca Twynham?"

Oh, the deep timbre of his voice did good things to her naughty places.

Zeke shrugged and that annoyed the hell out of her.

"Yes," she snapped. "Rebecca Twynham. Zeke said he'd take me to her." The phone she'd swiped buzzed in her pocket and it was echoed by a ding from the one in Zeke's. "And don't tell me she's not here. I, uh, *borrowed* a cell phone. I know all about this werewolf business and the HBIC and the fact that you're looking for me— I mean, Lorelei and Paisley. And that you have Rebecca. You got her into your weird magic cult thing you've got going on."

Hot Guy turned a glare on Zeke. "I'm assuming she had your phone."

"Yup." Zeke rocked back on his heels, hands tucked in his pockets and shoulders slouched as if it didn't matter.

"And she read your messages," Hot Guy snapped at Zeke and she decided she'd just refer to the man as Guy until he got around to introducing himself. She wasn't about to call him "D" like Zeke did.

"She just said she did." Zeke sighed and rolled his eyes before turning his attention to her. "And I said I'd get you to Rebecca. I didn't say when."

"Zeke," Guy's slow drawl had her focusing on him once again. Oh, it wasn't looking good, either. Not when she noticed his deeply tanned skin was kinda gray… and furry. "Tell me she's not who I think she is."

Zeke's grin was wide and she had the urge to kick him in the shin so it'd go away. "She's not who you think she is."

"You're lying," Guy growled.

"Yup."

"Zeke, we can't keep her—"

"Damn right you can't," Lorelei cut in, tired of them talking around her and not *to* her. "I feel like I'm a damned parrot with all this repeating, but you two aren't listening. I want Rebecca and Paisley and then I want out."

Anger continued to rise in her, burning her skin and the heat raced over her body. Damn stupid men. Damn stupid werewolves. Damn stupid whatever-the-fuck that brought her to this hoity-toity werewolf "Gathering." Damn it all.

Both men focused on her, eyebrows raised. Their gazes didn't remain on her eyes, but gently stroked her from head to toe.

Stupid hot bastards making her want them in very dirty, naughty ways.

And what the fuck was up with her wanting *them*. Not Zeke, not Guy, but both.

She didn't want to think about the fact that she'd always fantasized about banging two guys.

"Miss…" Guy raised his eyebrows.

"Miss Nothing. I don't know who the hell you are. Why should you know my name?"

Zeke stepped forward. "It's Back the Hell Up. I shortened it to just B."

He grinned and winked at Lorelei.

She pretended not to notice. She also pretended not to feel the way her body wanted to lean into him.

God, she needed to get laid. By non-furry, non-werewolf, non-hot guys not named Zeke or Guy.

Guy turned his attention to Zeke. "Didn't you introduce yourself?"

Zeke shrugged. "Only after she put that pink toy against my head."

Guy closed his eyes and took a slow breath. She noticed his lips moving and, based on their exchange, she figured he was probably praying for patience. At least, that's what her mother always did with her and her sisters.

"You've met Zeke. I'm Dylan Clarke." He pressed his hand to his chest, bringing her attention back to his sculpted body.

Lorelei swallowed hard, trying her best not to imagine what his skin would taste like or how wonderful it'd be to nibble her way down his abs… She tried and failed because a low whimper escaped.

That had Dylan growling low. "Sweet, you really shouldn't make those sounds."

She licked her lips and met his yellowed eyes and whined. "What sounds?"

"Damn, baby." Zeke's hoarse whisper reached her and she moaned.

The more they talked, the more she wanted them. What the fucking fuck?

Another shake overtook her, this one seeming to sink into her bones and jarring her from inside out. Her grip on her weapon faltered and she nearly lost her gun amidst the tremors.

"Lorelei?" Worry replaced the hint of desire she'd heard in Zeke's voice.

"Not," she wheezed, another vibration sending her wobbling. "Not Lore—"

"We know you are, sweet." Dylan took a step closer to her, decreasing the distance between them.

"Oh God," she burned. Fucking *burned.* Her skin, her muscles, everything inside her. "Stop talking."

"Baby?" Then Zeke moved beside Dylan.

Another round of vibrations assaulted her. "What's happening?"

She was on fire. Scorched by the heat and a rolling wave of desire kicked her ass with their every word, every syllable, every breath.

"Call Emmett and Levy," Dylan whispered.

"But—"

"Now," Sexy in Slacks snarled and she sucked in a rough breath.

"Stop. Talking." Another sound and she'd crumble.

It kept getting worse because now cool air blew over her skin, the gentle breeze sent drifting over her by the AC. It attempted to rid her of the growing agony, but it did something else, too. It brought her their scent. Wood and smoke and rain and… they were *werewolves*, but her body didn't give a damn.

"Dylan, they'll take her…"

Lorelei sobbed, her pink protection tumbling from her fingers, and she hugged herself. She wrapped her arms around her waist, clutching her sides as the cry was torn from her throat. She squeezed her eyes shut, praying for an end to whatever the hell was happening to her.

A rumbling growl vibrated the air, disturbing the cooling breeze and sending another agonizing wave of sensation down her spine. She fell to the ground, begging for the end. The change of position had her jeans and shirt scraping her skin, pushing another moan past her lips.

"Dammit, Zeke." The growl began anew and then the rapid thump of someone approaching reached her ears.

She fought for control of her body, pushed from the ground with all her might only to tumble down again. Her nerves burned, her muscles twitching and urging her to hug her knees close and pray that it'd end. The torture told her to fuck off.

A new warmth hovered near, the increase in temperature eased her rather than pushing more pain forward. It helped smooth some of her ragged edges and she drew in a harsh breath.

"Lorelei," Dylan crooned, softly and tenderly. "Easy, sweet."

His deep timbre didn't send another bolt of sobs through her. No, it drew forth other sensations. Ones that said she wanted his touch, wanted to taste him, wanted to revel in his body. Now she whimpered for an entirely different reason.

Some of the aching receded, letting her relax a bit, letting her breathe and open her eyes. She met Dylan's gaze, their eyes locked while Zeke's low voice danced along her spine. A bolt of pain-tinged desire assaulted her, but it was tempered by Dylan's presence.

"Just relax. That's it. Breathe with me, now." His words stroked her, brushing away even more of the unending agony.

His hands hovered over her, seeming stuck in the air, and her only thought was that she craved the feel of his skin on hers. Everything inside her screamed to take his hand and hold it close. To snatch Dylan to her and then hunt Zeke.

*Touch. Touch. Touch.*

Lorelei reached for him, her hand darting through the air and…

"Dylan, they said not to touch…"

She grabbed him, fingers wrapping around his wrist in a firm hold. One that was meant to capture him and keep him close. Dylan and Zeke and Dylan and…

Yes, her hand held Dylan captive.

Her glowing hand.

Her glowing hand now etched with swirling, intertwining marks that were a deeper gold.

Then the end of Zeke's statement reached Lorelei. "…her."

Dylan wasn't supposed to touch her? Why?

Then her question was answered in a rush of pain and pleasure that roared through her veins. It eclipsed every other sensation. The scrape of cloth and the searing ache were gone with the new, breathtaking pulse of energy that overtook her.

That took her down, down, down into unconsciousness where the pain couldn't reach her. And neither could the pleasure.

*

Zeke was too far away. He couldn't catch Lorelei, couldn't hold her close, couldn't do a fucking thing but watch her crumple to the ground in a boneless heap.

Then it hit him. No, *she* hit him. The burst of magic, of uncontrollable power, struck him in the chest. It wove into his body, creeping into every part of his soul and then a soothing warmth replaced that coldness in his heart.

The heat was followed by the body-enveloping light, blinding him to the world… to everything. He saw her then, saw her very essence, and ached to soothe the ragged heartache that filled her from head to toe.

"Zeke? Dammit, Zeke! What the fuck is going on?" He recognized Emmett's voice coming through the cell phone, the Ruling Warden's worry palpable, but whatever was going on robbed him of speech.

The glow filled the room, blasting over every surface and enclosing him and Dylan. Was this what happened when Wardens found their mate?

The brightness continued, pulsing from Lorelei's inert body. Pleasure at finding her singed his nerves and brought arousal rushing forward.

She was theirs and this… had something to do with that. He knew Whitney, the Ruling Wardens' mate, dimly glowed when she was angry. Had this happened to the woman when she came in contact with her mates?

"Zeke! Don't touch her. No matter what— Oh, fuck," Emmett groaned. "I felt it. One of you did."

Zeke didn't. Dylan did. Dylan, his Warden partner, was currently touching their mate, his wrist captured in her small hand and a bolt of jealousy hit him. But the emotion didn't linger. No, it was brushed aside by the ethereal light that emanated from Lorelei. It was as if she spoke to him, telling him there was no reason to be jealous. The push reminded him that she *was* Warden Born and *was* meant to mate two Wardens: him and Dylan.

He dropped the phone, uncaring that it bounced against the end table before clattering to the ground. No, it didn't matter when every cell urged him to go to her. No, to go to them. His wolf howled in approval and his magic sang with the need to grasp her other hand. He wanted that bright light to encompass all three of them.

Zeke refused to let anything get in the way of his desires. A wave of his hand discarded the furniture between him and Dylan and Lorelei. The couch went tumbling over the carpet, the small end tables doing the same while the lamp crashed against the wall. There, his path was clear. Nothing hindered his course and his strides ate up the ground between them.

Dylan was on her right and he knelt at her left, reaching for her.

Dylan tried to stop him. "Zeke, didn't they say—"

He snarled at his partner and grasped her free hand, encasing it with his own and then… Bliss. There was no other way to describe the sensations. Bliss and joy and need and an overwhelming need to kill anyone who dared separate them.

Theirs. Theirs. Theirs.

A shadow broke through the brightness, lurking closer and casting itself over their small group.

"I told you not to touch her, dammit." The rumbling voice cut into their peace and Lorelei trembled, twitching and jerking in their embrace.

When a large, rough hand gripped his shoulder, his response was immediate. His response? No, his *wolf's* response was instantaneous.

Human teeth were replaced with the beast's and he turned his head, snapping at the male attempting to pull him from his mate. Tangy blood filled his mouth, and the animal both rejoiced and gagged. It was happy they'd hurt the intruding male, but they only wanted one person's coppery fluid in their mouth: Lorelei's.

He spat the offending liquid on the floor, uncaring if it stained the carpet. The intruder backed away with a snarl, but Zeke ignored the male. He was no longer a threat to his mating.

"I thought you told him not to touch her." Another male was in the room… Levy. The other Ruling Warden.

"Of course I fucking told him. You think I wanted this to happen?" Emmett snarled.

Zeke wanted this to happen. Whatever *this* was. It brought him closer to Lorelei. Closer and closer with each passing second. It was as if their three souls reached and stretched for each other, beckoning them closer.

"Well, we have to separate them," Levy sighed.

Dylan was the one to respond this time, and it was immediate. His partner lashed out, not with fang and claw, but with pure power. Then he realized the longer they remained connected, the stronger their magic became. It stretched and flexed, filling all three of them with a Warden's abilities. Only it wasn't the familiar rush, but something more. Much, much more.

Two low grunts reached him and he imagined the Ruling Wardens colliding with the wall. That wasn't far enough away, not hardly, but he wasn't about to release her in order to rid them of the two males completely. As long as they kept their distance, everything would be fine.

The soft click of the door teased his ear, but it was the fresh scent of spring rain that drew his attention. It was so like Lorelei's but different. Where Lorelei was sweet honeysuckle, this newcomer was… soothing lavender.

The voice that immediately followed confirmed his suspicions. "You two just had to do this yourselves, didn't you? You couldn't wait two seconds for me to come along."

Whitney. Ruling Warden Mate. She knew what was going on. She knew and she wasn't a threat to them. She wouldn't try to claim Lorelei and she wasn't strong enough to steal her from their grasp.

The female padded forward, her shadow eventually breaking past the blinding light. Her long brown hair flowed past her shoulders, the dark hue contrasting with her own halo of gold.

Whitney crouched near Lorelei's head and Zeke focused on the woman. "Hey, guys. How's it going?"

She extended her hands over Lorelei's head. Her fingers twitched, but she didn't attempt to touch their mate.

Zeke took a moment to glance at Dylan and take in his partner's reaction to Whitney's presence. He found the male wasn't staring at Whitney, but at something beyond the woman. He followed Dylan's line of sight and squinted to see past the glow, watching as Emmett and Levy lifted themselves from the ground.

Dylan curled his lip and bared a fang, growling low.

Of course the sound had the energy from Lorelei flaring, sending a threatening wave of magic through the air. It sent a bolt of arousal and need into Zeke's body, but it knocked Emmett and Levy back on their asses.

Their mate was protecting them even as she lay unconscious.

"Hey," Whitney bit off the word and snapped her fingers in front of Dylan's face. "You need to chill out. I can't help you two if you keep doing that."

Dylan narrowed his eyes at Whitney but remained silent.

The Ruling Warden Mate sat on her heels and her gaze went from Lorelei to Zeke, then Dylan and back to their mate. "Okay, you're not going to like this, but you need to let go."

It was Zeke's turn to snarl and Lorelei's unconscious reaction was instantaneous, knocking the two Ruling Wardens to the ground once again. Even Whitney swayed with that push of power.

"Damn, she's got a punch, huh?" Whitney shook her head. "Look, you don't understand what's going on, but the longer you two hold her, the longer this will go on. You need to let her come around and have everything explained. Then the three of you will deal with things." She waved toward Lorelei. "Right now, the best thing for her is to give her body a rest. You guys were born Wardens. You can control your magic. She cannot. She's not gonna power down unless you let go."

Zeke looked to his partner, ready to take a cue from his longtime friend. They'd been through so much shit together... If D was onboard, he'd fight his instincts and release their mate.

Yellow eyes met his and after several seconds ticked past, Dylan finally nodded.

Agreeing was the easy part. Doing was a different story...

He returned his gaze to Lorelei, studying her heart-shaped face and the hazel eyes currently hidden from him. Would they spark with anger? Or need? He'd sensed her arousal as the power took control. Would she turn it on them once she realized how her life had just changed?

Probably.

He hoped she didn't kick his ass too hard.

Zeke battled his wolf, growling at the animal when it refused to budge. Then he finally beat it into submission. He captured the beast and forced it into his mental cage. They had to do this for Lorelei. He needed to remember that.

Even as he released her and the pain of loss struck him in his chest, he had to remember…

Zeke's fingertips lifted from her wrist, their skin no longer connected through touch, and he saw Dylan did the same. The instant the link was destroyed, the glow eased. It lessened until it merely hovered around Lorelei. As if it was a protective shell, keeping others from coming near.

A force field.

He'd been watching way too many Star Trek reruns.

"See? That wasn't so hard." Whitney was way too perky now.

And yes, it was hard. His entire being called for her touch and yet he'd released her. Dylan rumbled, the sound vibrating the air and the low glow surrounding Lorelei flared higher, reaching for them both.

"Okay, see that right there?" Whitney pointed at the way Lorelei's power wrapped around their wrists. "That's a very bad thing. So you're gonna back away and those two are gonna pop her up to—"

It was Zeke's turn to voice his objection. "*Ours.*"

Lorelei's magic crept along their arms, inching higher.

Whitney stared at the ceiling. "God save me from possessive Wardens." She huffed and lowered her head. "Okay, let's rethink this. You two can't carry her. You're not allowed to touch her anymore. What we *can* do is one of you will go with Emmett and Levy. The other will stay with me and Lorelei and I'll transport you there myself. No nasty boys will touch her. Are we okay with that?"

No, he was very not okay with that. But it was necessary because beneath the healthy brightness of her magic, her skin was paling more and more.

"Dylan will stay." His partner was the stronger of them and could protect her for the split second he was parted from Lorelei.

"Whitney, we're not leaving you here." Emmett's tone was smooth, but the threat was evident in his gaze.

"Emmett, I don't interfere with your job. I let the two of you handle your Wardens as you see fit, but I have this." Whitney glanced over her shoulder. "As males, you don't get this. You need to listen to me."

Zeke could tell the Ruling Warden didn't like what Whitney said, but he finally jerked his head in a quick nod.

That had Zeke staring at Dylan. "You'll take care of her."

"You know I will."

"We're right behind you. We're going right to the Ruling Alpha's suite." Whitney reached toward him, but stopped just shy of touching his skin. "She's my cousin, Zeke. I can feel it. I'm not about to let something happen to her. Their suite is the safest place in the hotel. The second you disappear, we'll be there."

Zeke understood her words and even accepted them as truth, but…

"The faster you leave, the faster we get her help, Z." Dylan's words were a hoarse whisper. He noted the man's fur coating his arms and the sharp edge of his jaw. Dylan held onto his human shape by force of will alone.

No longer hesitating, he pushed to his feet and strode toward Emmett and Levy. He didn't pause, didn't falter, and immediately reached for one of the Ruling Wardens as soon as he was close enough.

His arm closed over Levy's shoulder, fingers curving over the man's flesh, and then the hotel room disappeared in a flare of light. The brightness only lasted a brief moment, a single blink before they were sucked into the darkness. It enveloped them, wrapping them in a choking, midnight blanket. It ripped the air from his lungs, and strangled him with its fierce grip. He thought he'd suffocate before all was said and done, die in the middle of the dark that surrounded him.

Then, just as quickly as it began, it ended with him collapsing on the heavy carpeted floor of another suite. One he imagined belonged to the Ruling Alphas.

Shouts surrounded him, growls and snarls came from all sides, but he didn't give a damn. He waited for his partner and his mate.

And waited.

And waited.

And waited…

*

Dylan couldn't tear his gaze from Lorelei. Their Lorelei.

The magic that lived inside her continued to pulse and press against her skin while the marks covering her body flared over her flesh. He'd never imagined… He'd read the announcement from the Ruling Wardens. He'd even seen Whitney in the flesh and heard the words from the Ruling Warden Mate. Yet he hadn't believed.

He let his hand hover over Lorelei's skin and desire bloomed in his chest as her power reached for him. Tendrils of light kissed his skin, wrapping around his fingers and seeming to draw him to her.

Until another grip halted his progress. The fingers encircling his wrist glowed brighter than his mate, the throb of magic overwhelming Lorelei's gentle tugs.

"Maybe you didn't understand. No. Touching." Whitney spat the words through gritted teeth and then he noticed… It wasn't anger that had her growling at him. No, it was fatigue and worry and… fear.

"What's happening, Whitney?" He withdrew his hand, fighting his mate's beckoning power.

"It's too much, too fast. There's a reason Tests of Proximity with Wardens are closely monitored. There's a reason Warden Born are gently activated before the tests even begin. It's so something like this doesn't happen." She sighed and her attention drifted to Lorelei. "It's burning her from inside out, Dylan. The more contact, the more it hurts her. You gotta let my guys and Miles and Holden work on her before she comes out of it."

Miles and Holden, Dylan's rage overtook him, the anger rising hard and fast. They were Wardens, males responsible for verifying a human female's status as a Warden Born before they were introduced to other Wardens. He'd seen them meet with the humans drawn to the Gathering. Seen them *touch* the women.

"No," he snarled and Lorelei's magic flared, the shimmering wisps stretching toward him.

"Dylan," Whitney sighed. "What's more important to you? Healing Lorelei or losing her. That's what we're faced with right now. Choose."

He swallowed past the lump in his throat. Choose? Wasn't there a door number three? Apparently not. "Heal her."

Whitney jerked her head in a quick nod. "Okay, the teleporting thing is new to me, but I can get us there. I'm gonna hold on to her, you're gonna hold on to me." She gave him a rueful grin. "A little power boost would be great, but be prepared to get a punch to the jaw from one of my mates for your trouble. The good thing is, the other one is getting better at healing."

Dylan grabbed Whitney without question. Teleportation wasn't one of his skills, but he was thankful the Ruling Warden Mate had the ability.

"Ready?" Whitney raised her eyebrows.

"Yeah."

"Hold on tight." With that, the woman grasped Lorelei's wrist and closed her eyes.

A second ticked past, and then two, and he wondered if Whitney truly could accomplish her goal.

He shouldn't have doubted her. Not when the dim glow in the room flared to life and encompassed them in a wall of pure white. That brightness was immediately followed by darkness. Not the nothingness of midnight, but a deeper, blacker existence. Air rushed from his lungs and he couldn't draw in another breath. His body betrayed him, heart refusing to beat and muscles refusing to tense. He was frozen and yet… moving? The rush of the wind was unmistakable, the noise filling his ears. But his hair wasn't stirred by the breeze.

The gloom continued, remaining in place as second after second passed and he wondered if it'd ever end, if they'd ever reach their destination.

Then… then midnight slowly receded, the delicate light of the hotel room gradually appearing and replacing the black. It was slow and a new tremor wracked him, the vibration shaking his body. No, it was Whitney shaking, trembles overtaking her small frame.

Then more sound reached him… Lorelei's whimpers and whines coming on the heels of Whitney's hoarse cries.

"No. Wrong. Stop it." The brightness increased, finally giving him a clear look at the Ruling Warden Mate, and shock and fear held him captive.

The woman always had a gentle glow about her, her pale skin a hint lighter than the average person. She wasn't just fair, she was luminous. Her power made her appear otherworldly and it was a comforting, soothing hue.

This was not *that.* Whitney was pure white, not even the darker color of her marks visible. She wasn't just painted with power, she was the embodiment of magic. She turned to him, white eyes boring into him, and the words boomed from her mouth. Not the lyrical tones that were familiar to him. No, this was power at its base and it throbbed through this hidden place.

"This is wrong."

The message slammed into him, pummeling him with every syllable until he was sure his bones were crushed beneath their weight.

He didn't know what was wrong, what had set Whitney off, but she was staring at him as if he could fix it. Instead of answering or begging for an explanation, he dug into himself and threw his magic at her, feeding her what he could. He felt sure she could repair whatever had gone wrong if she had enough power to feed her.

He was mistaken. So very, very mistaken.

That lightness pulsed and grew, revealing their destination. Only… it wasn't what they'd aimed for. Dylan was familiar with the hotel's décor. The attempts at soothing colors and delicate decorations.

That wasn't what slowly came into focus.

No, it was dirty, grimy, and run down. The flooring that had once been a light brown was caked with God knew what. The walls were yellowed by cigarette smoke and the furniture was no more than cracked milk cartons with pieces of wood atop them.

That… that worried him.

But what terrified him was the fact that three wolves stared at their small group. Saliva dripped from their jaws, white fangs gleaming in the dim light, and their fur stood on end. An air of anticipation surrounded them and he knew they waited for them. Waited and craved their blood, ready to pounce the moment they fully materialized.

A fourth person stepped into view, standing tall and holding an aged book in his hands. His lips moved as if he read from the tome and it wasn't until he raised his gaze that true fear struck Dylan.

Eyes so like his own stared back at him.

*No.*

The male grinned and a message was planted in Dylan's mind. One word.

*Yes.*

The man's attention shifted to the woman before him. Not Whitney. No, he followed his line of sight to Lorelei. His Lorelei.

Whitney whimpered and he noticed one tremble and then two and then more wrack her body. She was losing against their attacker, his rapid repetition of the spell overriding Whitney's efforts.

No, he wouldn't let the man win.

Ignoring the Ruling Warden Mate's orders, he grasped Lorelei. He reached for his mate, wrapped his fingers around her arm and drew on the growing power that pulsed through her. It throbbed and punched its way into his body. It seared his veins as it traveled over his nerves and then he felt it slam into Whitney.

The Ruling Warden Mate screamed, the sound breaking into Dylan's mind and he even saw the wolves and single male wince with the shout. That cringe was the last thing he saw before the dark stole him once again. It ripped them away from their would-be attackers and plunged them into midnight.

Less than a heartbeat later, light burst over them, throwing them from the airless darkness into bright hues.

Unsure of where they'd emerged, he reacted first and decided he'd apologize later. He roared, the change whipping through him in a blinding rush and he knew Lorelei's magic spurred him to go even faster.

Clothes were burned away by the speed of his shift and rush of power, and he was quick to maneuver Whitney until she was atop Lorelei, leaving him to easily stand over the two women. He pulled his lips back, exposing his teeth as a rumbling, threatening growl escaped his muzzle. Whoever lingered would go through him to get to the females.

A sting hit him, blossoming in his chest, and he merely absorbed the pain, allowing it to flow over him in a gentle wave. The pain was nothing if it meant keeping the females from harm. He would gladly take it and more.

Roars and growls surrounded him, attacking from all sides, but it was merely those annoying stings and jabs that came forward.

Slowly the blinding light from Whitney and Lorelei eased, drawing into the women to reveal… A suite similar to his own, only this one was filled with familiar males and females.

Most importantly, Zeke. Zeke was there, half shifted, and his partner's gaze flitted from wolf to wolf. He jerked and flexed and it was then that not only did the Ruling Alphas hold his friend physically captive, but Miles and Holden captured him with their magic as well.

Another rush of pain caused him to wince and he swung his gaze toward the source. Emmett and Levy. The Ruling Wardens were focused on him, their bodies flush with their magic. He suddenly realized the aches assaulting him came from those two. Another bolt flew through the air and he snapped at it with his jaws, his power using the wolf's intent and disseminating it before it struck him.

"Dylan!" Zeke's yell was followed by a snarl and then a grunt that had him refocusing on his partner. He noticed that Keller, one of the Ruling Alphas, sported a bloody nose. "You need to chill, man. I know it was scary, but you need to relax and let Whitney up. No one here is gonna hurt her or Lorelei, okay?"

Dylan let his glare hit each of the room's occupants. He would kill them if they tried to injure either of the females.

"C'mon, D. You need to relax," Zeke coaxed and he shot a questioning look to his partner. "I promise.

They're gonna help our mate. The whole teleporting thing isn't fun, but you gotta let them through."

*Isn't fun?*

Talk about an understatement. No, it definitely hadn't been fun.

And Dylan was fairly sure he knew why. Someone found a way to highjack their trip from the tenth floor to the Ruling Alpha's suite.

No, it wasn't just someone…

It was the patriarch of the eldest of the five families. Their line could be traced back a millennia. The male he saw now led his esteemed line and demanded blind obedience. So much like his father who perished last year at the hands of the Ruling Wardens and Whitney.

Yes, the wolf was very like his father.

Or rather, *their* father.

# Chapter Four

Lorelei's body throbbed with every beat of her heart—hands pulsing and muscles clenching with each thump. She was conscious of each compression and every breath that slipped in and out of her lungs. Her nerves were alive and waiting for stimulation, on edge with anticipation of… something. She wasn't sure what. She did know something, though. Pain no longer pummeled her with invisible hands while searing heat encompassed her.

She forced her eyes open, demanding her lids part and reveal the world. It took time, a demand or two, but the sticky eyelids finally separated. The grit and grime that came with waking covered her lashes and she instinctively brought her hand to her face.

Then she was reminded of why she was sleeping. The brightness she remembered was now a barely-there glow, but it lingered. As did the swirling marks that marred her skin. Each one was exactly like the next. Some larger, some smaller, but they were present.

She flipped her hand over, staring at the back and the gentle progression of the new texture as it went from hand to wrist to forearm and on until it disappeared beneath her top.

A top she didn't recognize. She frowned, eyebrows lowering and coming together. The small movement stung, but that didn't keep her from scowling at the fabric.

How… What…

She must have made some sort of sound because then a vaguely familiar woman was there, her presence filling her vision. Worry-filled dark brown eyes met hers, anxiousness and concern warring across her features.

"Hey, how are you feeling?" The words pounded through her mind and she moaned, squeezing her eyes shut against the sensations. The stranger winced. "That bad, huh? Okay." She raised her hands and Lorelei spotted symbols similar to her own coating the other woman's skin. "I'm gonna touch you real lightly and real slow and your magic isn't gonna kick my ass, okay?"

Magic?

Wha—

Lorelei wasn't able to finish thinking about her question before hands were on her. And something inside Lorelei reacted. It surged forward, pressing and stretching her skin until she thought she'd pop like a balloon.

"Yeah, your magic isn't paying attention, hon. Maybe you can calm your heart a little and I'll take some of this pain away." The woman shoved the words past her gritted teeth.

Calm. She could almost do calm. Especially if calming meant this pain would cease. Lorelei didn't even pretend to understand what the hell had happened to her, but she was all for putting an end to some of it.

So she looked into herself, closed her eyes, and sought the peacefulness that tended to remain just out of reach. She drew that safe and soothing feeling forward and sent it sliding through her body. She willed her muscles to unclench and ease as she slowed her breathing. With each new part of her that unclenched, more of the pain receded.

Thank God for yoga.

"That's it." The stranger sighed and her relief allowed Lorelei to calm further.

Soothed, she was able to explore her surroundings with her gaze. She lay atop a huge bed, the mattress massive and she realized it was easily king sized. Which meant the room was definitely big enough to hold something so massive. She let her stare travel further to the small sitting area off to the side, to the large dressers and the door that stood ajar to reveal the bathroom. A set of double doors was to the bathroom's left, both snug and shut tight. The colors and patterns in the blanket's fabric as well as the paintings that graced the walls told her she was still in the hotel.

"Where," the word was hoarse and Lorelei cleared her throat. "Where am I? What's going on? Why are you people doing this to me?"

"Oh, Lorelei." The woman sighed and the soft click of a door unlatching cut off whatever she was about to say.

The panel swung open, just enough for a familiar face to peek past the opening. "I heard voices."

Lorelei's heart clenched and her lungs burned. Her eyes stung from new tears and she swallowed back a sob that threatened to explode from her chest. "Rebecca."

Her sister. Her baby sister.

Rebecca eased into the room and gently swung the door shut behind her before padding toward Lorelei. "Hey, Lor." Her sister stopped beside the bed and then took the stranger's place at Lorelei's side. "You stepped in it this time, huh?"

"Rebecca, we have to get out of here. We have to find a way out. I found this phone and the things it said and those guys…" She didn't fight to stop the tears, letting one after another trail down her cheek. And then… then she voiced the words that made her a coward, but she was beyond caring. The fear, the pain, the overwhelming stress made her put voice to her emotions. There is no courage without fear. "I'm scared."

"Oh, Lor-Lor. I was too, but it's okay. I promise."

Lorelei shook her head. "No, the texts and emails. *Werewolves,* Rebecca. And it hurt so bad and the light and…"

She shuddered. She'd managed to look composed, to keep her head on straight, but she needed a chance to fall apart. Then she could put herself back together.

"Hush." Rebecca enveloped Lorelei's hand with her own. "Hush, now. We're gonna talk about all this. Remember when I was burned? When I was three? And you held my hand and you told me everything would be okay. That you'd protect me and I'd always be safe because you wouldn't let anything happen to me ever again."

Lorelei nodded. She remembered that time. Little three-year-old Rebecca got caught in a fire that burned her from ribs to upper thighs. Lorelei spent months at her sister's side. Reading to her, playing games, and even when her mom told her to go to sleep, she'd always crawl into her youngest sister's bed. She'd carefully hug Rebecca and promise everything would be okay. She promised.

"I promise you're safe. I *promise.*" Rebecca echoed Lorelei's thoughts.

Her sister glanced over her shoulder and called to the stranger. "Whitney?" The woman, Whitney, came closer and sat behind Rebecca, but still visible to Lorelei. "Lor, I want you to listen. I want you to listen and look at your hand and realize what you're hearing is real. It's the truth."

Truth.

Lorelei looked at her hand, at the halo of light that hovered above her skin. Then she looked at the matching glimmer that encompassed Whitney.

"Okay." She swallowed past the ball of emotion clouding her throat. "Okay, I'll listen."

And she did listen.

Lorelei listened as Whitney—*her cousin*—explained about werewolves. Told her there were stronger wolves, those that were different because of their dominance or ability to wield magic, and they weren't like regular werewolves.

Alpha Pairs and Warden Pairs.

Alphas needed a female to keep their dominance in check and those human women carried a Mark on their skin. Wardens required a shared mate to strengthen them, but they didn't have visible Marks until they met their mates.

At one point, it was thought that Warden Pairs didn't have mates, but in truth, they were hidden by a twisting perversion of magic. Now, they were revealed and summoned to the Gathering.

Whitney was the mate of the Ruling Wardens.

Rebecca was mated to two alphas.

"You have a Mark?" Lorelei kept her attention on Rebecca and tension filled her sister's features.

"Yes, it was… destroyed in the fire."

Lorelei squeezed her sister's hand. "Oh, Rebecca…"

"It was on purpose, Lor." A tear trailed down Rebecca's face and her sister brushed it away. "No one knew about Warden Born women, but our family has a history of producing Alpha Marked girls. Grandma had a bad mating and…" Rebecca brushed another droplet from her face. "They burned me on purpose. If they'd known about Warden Born, I'm sure they would have done something to you and Paisley as well."

Lorelei felt the words as if they were a physical blow to her gut. "You're sure? I mean, that they… and me and Paisley are…"

"I have no doubt. They sent…" Rebecca trembled. "Some of the Wardens are better at certain things than others. A set was dispatched to speak with our family last night." Her sister nodded. "It— The fire was set on purpose. They put something on my skin to ensure that part of me was nearly destroyed."

Lorelei was tugged back to the past, to Rebecca's soaked bandages and tears and the pain that filled a three-year-old girl. Then on to the way she'd always hung back, how she lived a half-life because the scarring made her so self-conscious. And the way Grandma always glared at Rebecca. Glared at her little sister as if she'd gladly see her dead.

Lorelei wasn't one to hold onto hate, but right then, right there, it was nothing but hate pumping and throbbing through her veins. It demanded she hunt that old woman down and tear her into tiny pieces. What kind of person did that?

"Whoa, let's slow that roll there…" Whitney drew her attention and the woman's gaze met Lorelei's before lowering to her arms. Lorelei's glowing and pulsating arms. "We need to be real easy. You're exhausted from being brought here, hiding and then finding the guys. Raging homicidal desires won't help anything."

Lorelei fought for calm as Whitney asked, searching within herself and hunting for a soothing thought. One image sprung to mind, the two men standing side by side in that hotel room. Zeke and Dylan. Sexy as all get out and complete opposites. She kinda liked that about them.

"It doesn't matter anymore, Lor. I have Aidan and Carson and…" Rebecca gave Lorelei a gentle squeeze. "And we found you. Now we just need to find Paisley and it'll be perfect."

"Paisley… You're sure she's here?" Lorelei didn't want to think about how frightened their middle sister might be.

Rebecca nodded. "Yeah, two of the Wardens are good at finding people and they… They knew you were here and so is Paisley. Since we know you're Warden Born and Paisley doesn't have a Mark, we're assuming she's Warden Born, too."

God, this was so much to take in. "Let's assume I believe you. What's next? I mean… I can't go walking around like a glow stick."

Rebecca tore her attention from Lorelei and focused on Whitney. "I'm gonna let you handle that one."

Whitney grumbled, "Fine, give me the hard stuff." The woman huffed. "Remember how Warden Born don't get glowy until they find their mates? And what should have happened was that you would meet with a pair of Wardens who would give your power a nudge to confirm you're really Warden Born. Then you would have been given some time to settle a little before meeting Warden Pairs. Basically a jump start and then letting you rest in an idle before revving your engines." Whitney raised the corner of her mouth up in a small grin. "Instead, you went straight to engines revving and with everything that happened, you were knocked out when your mates touched you."

Mates.

Touched.

Her.

"I have mates?" She ignored the way her voice trembled.

"Yeah," Rebecca's single word was followed by a slow nod.

"Two of them? I'm Warden Born and you're telling me I found my mates?"

Twin nods from Whitney and Rebecca.

Lorelei's mind raced, spinning from one corner to another as she replayed the last day and a half. She'd only come into contact with two particular wolves.

"And they are…?" She let the question dangle, holding her breath as she waited for the answer.

"You know who they are, Lorelei." Whitney's words were soft.

Yeah, she had a good idea, she just didn't want to accept it.

"I don't…" She licked her suddenly dry lips, fighting for words that wouldn't come. She squeezed Rebecca's hand, tightening her hold and searching for calm. She watched the glow increase, a grid of color rising above her skin. "I'm not ready."

So very, very not ready.

Werewolves.

Magic.

Her family.

When her issues were placed side by side, Lorelei had to admit that she had more trouble with her family's actions than the existence of werewolves and magic. Maybe there was something inside her that had always called for them. Something that knew they were real and was just waiting for her to get a clue.

"You don't have to be ready right this second." Rebecca stroked Lorelei's hand with her thumb. "But I will warn you that you'll be very drawn to them. You'll want to, *you know*, immediately. It's part of who they are and who you are. You can fight, but your body is going to urge you to get busy."

Get busy. Right. She'd already felt some of that, hadn't she?

Whitney picked up where Rebecca left off. "It'll be worse because your power is calling to theirs. It's another dimension to your mating that Rebecca didn't experience. Keep in mind that what's driving you toward them is also pushing them to you. And," Whitney paused a moment as if gathering her thoughts. "And it's gonna start out biological. Your bodies will do the talking for you. But once you get past that part, once you three take the edge off, you'll realize it's not just your magic tying you together. You'll see they were made for you, Lorelei. Just like you were made for them." Whitney's glowing gaze met hers. "They're yours and you can make it beautiful if you let it."

Beautiful.

*Three.*

Lorelei let her eyes drift closed and thought of Zeke's long hair and sparkling eyes. Thought of Dylan's crisp appearance and the strength that lived in every carved muscle.

"It's Zeke and Dylan, isn't it? Those are the only two..."

"They seem to think so." Whitney spoke, her voice still low.

"No, they're right. I'm just…" Scared. She was just scared. "Are they still here? Should I… Do they want to… I can't…"

Rebecca leaned over her, giving Lorelei a tight hug. "You can do anything. You're stronger than all three of us put together. And I know they want to see you. Whitney's mates have kept them back, but they want to check on you. I think Emmett finally did something to Zeke so he couldn't talk."

Something inside Lorelei flexed and then the glow flared, slicing through the air and encompassing her and her sister in the pulsing ball. The power was pissed. No, beyond pissed that someone would do something to a male that belonged to them. He was theirs. *Theirs.*

Just like Dylan.

A single world popped to her lips and she fought to keep it back.

But it wouldn't be denied.

"*Mine.*"

*

Zeke listened to the Ruling Alpha Pair—Keller and Madden—with half an ear. The remainder of his attention was on the double doors firmly shut against him and Dylan. She was there, their mate was on the other side of those two wooden panels and the men sitting before them wouldn't let them near her.

"Zeke," Madden snarled at him and he forced himself to focus on the large alpha.

The man was enormous and an air of menace and power clung to him like a second skin. But at the moment, Zeke didn't give a damn. He'd use every ounce of his magic fighting the male if it meant getting to Lorelei.

"I'm listening," he grumbled.

He still only half paid attention. Lorelei was in that room and they were in the living room. How could they protect her from so far away?

"If you're listening, then you won't mind speaking and telling us why the hell my mate's cousin is unconscious in the other room," Keller snarled.

The sound was definitely a threat, but if there weren't things he feared more than the alpha, he definitely would have cowered. As it was, he was more scared of losing Lorelei. Everything else paled in comparison.

Zeke turned his head and truly looked at the alpha. "She's not."

The soft rustle of cloth, the change in her breathing, told Zeke she was conscious. The soft sounds were nearly inaudible, but he caught them. Grabbed them and held them close. She was awake. She was alive. That was all that mattered.

“Excuse me?” Another hint of menace filled Keller’s tone.

“Our mate is in there, but she’s not unconscious.”

Dylan gripped Zeke’s knee, nails transforming to a wolf’s sharpened tips and digging into his jeans. Damn man was gonna ruin another pair. “Z?”

“She’s awake, D. I haven’t heard her speak yet, but she’s up.”

Dylan released the breath he’d been holding in a great whoosh.

Keller tilted his head to the side, probably listening and trying to catch what Zeke heard. Silence surrounded them for a moment before the alpha finally nodded his head in agreement.

“Okay, she at least made it past that round.” It was Keller’s turn to release a relieved sigh. “Now we can worry about the rest.”

“The rest?” Dylan’s hold eased and he withdrew his hand.

Zeke glanced at his leg and noted the red stain that marred his pants. “Fucker, these were my favorite pair.”

“Why, because they haven’t been washed in a week?” Dylan drawled, the same annoying, teasing tone he’d been using for years.

Maybe things would work out.

"Dick. I've had these for years," he snarled back, falling into their old pattern.

The low click of a lock unlatching interrupted and the Ruling Wardens entered the space. The air around them crackled and snapped with power. The two men—Emmett and Levy—had their magic hovering near them the moment Lorelei went into their care. The Wardens lowered onto the loveseat beside the couch where the Alphas rested. Four powerful men against them. Four wolves who wanted to keep them away from Lorelei.

Zeke didn't think they could make it past the males, but they'd go down fighting.

"Miles and Holden are restarting their search and going floor by floor," Emmett murmured, and Zeke knew the Warden spoke about the hunt for Paisley. "It's hard because…"

Because the males were used to hunting for people on an even plane. At most, they'd travel up one or two floors when they hunted. Nearly twenty stories were hard on the wolves. Now, after confirming that Lorelei was Warden Born, they were anxious to find Paisley before she came into contact with her mates. No one wanted a repeat of Lorelei's reaction to Zeke and Dylan. He couldn't blame them for their anxiety. He wouldn't wish this worry on anyone.

"Thank them and if they need more help, if they need anything, tell them to send word." Madden was quick to break in.

Levy shot him and Dylan an unreadable look before turning back to the Ruling Alphas. "They could use blood. That hasn't changed."

Zeke frowned. "I'm not aware of any spells that require blood other than the darker magics. Like…"

He didn't need to finish his statement. They all knew blood magic was what once hid Warden Born from the Wardens and erased all knowledge of the women.

"That is still the case," Levy nodded. "But the nature of their abilities typically requires touch and a little concentration. At minimum, a hint of the person's scent."

"But?" Dylan voiced Zeke's thought.

"But with the conditions, all the wolves, the various floors, the people coming in and out of every room… If they had some blood, they'd be able to find her quicker." Levy's tone was grim and it took a moment for the Warden's words to make sense in his mind.

"No." Zeke barked out the word and he wasn't surprised to find it echoed by Dylan.

"No one is touching Lorelei. Take Rebecca's if you have to have their blood. Or even one of the Wickham sisters. Not Lorelei." Dylan's tone was as flat and unbending as Zeke felt.

"Rebecca's mates won't allow Miles and Holden near her." Emmett sighed. "And I doubt she knows that she could hold the key to finding Paisley." The wolf leveled a fierce glare at them both. "Do you want to be the one to tell them that their sister vanished because you couldn't push past your own possessiveness?"

"And what about Rebecca's mates?" Zeke growled back. "They can't push past theirs?"

"Rebecca's mates have an excuse. She was almost taken yesterday and their wolves still haven't calmed enough to leave her unprotected. Even now, one lurks at the entrance from the Ruling Warden suite to the Ruling Alpha suite," Keller gestured toward the opposite hallway where a set of spiral stairs led to the floor below, "while the other guards the main door. I can understand their reluctance to see even the smallest cut on her skin. But what's your excuse? Lorelei is injured through your own arrogance and inability to follow simple directions. Yes, she was unconscious, but it wasn't as if you'd lose her forever. It just meant she'd be out a little longer."

Dylan snorted and then released a mocking laugh. "Almost taken? No excuse?" His partner shook his head. "Oh, we have an excuse. Zeke just doesn't know it yet." The wolf drew in a deep breath and released it in a slow sigh. "It's a good thing we touched her, you know. If we hadn't," Dylan focused on the Ruling Wardens and Zeke noticed the flare of power coming from his partner.

Zeke took a moment to survey their surroundings. There was no danger lurking in the corners. Hell, at this point, no one would dare come near them. With so many alphas and Wardens in the small area… it'd be suicide.

"If we hadn't, both women would be gone. Or, at minimum, Lorelei." Dylan rested his hands on his knees, palms up. "If I hadn't touched her, she'd be gone and we'd have never found her. Just like Paisley, she'd be a ghost in the wind."

He frowned. "D, what the hell are you talking about?"

Yellow eyes met Zeke's and he knew that look, knew that his partner was about to reveal something that'd shake him to his bones.

"I'm saying that—" Dylan narrowed his eyes. "How long did you wait for us to appear?" His friend turned to the Ruling Wardens. "How many seconds?"

Levy frowned. "Ten maybe? No more than fifteen. I assumed Whitney had a hard time getting the journey started. She's strong enough to carry a half-dozen wolves, but it can take her a little while to begin. I figured it was worth waiting a few seconds to get Lorelei here rather than fight you two so we could transport her ourselves."

Dylan flashed a rueful grin and Zeke wondered what he was missing. "No, she had no problem starting. She did have an issue mid-transport."

"D?" He prodded his partner's shoulder while anxiety flooded Zeke's veins. His emotions fed off Dylan's and he knew that worry plagued the other male. "What the hell are you talking about?"

"I'm talking about," Dylan's words were slow and measured. "Someone tried to snatch the three of us out of the darkness before we got here. I'm saying Whitney was a glowing mass of pure magic when we landed because she drew on everything she had to stop them and it wasn't working. Lorelei has been out for so long because I took from her to keep those men from getting us all."

The words struck Zeke's chest, digging into his heart and squeezing the muscle until he felt as if it'd burst. Someone tried to take his mate and partner mid-teleport? No. That couldn't be.

"Is that even possible?" He tore his gaze from Dylan and looked to the Ruling Wardens.

"Obviously," Dylan muttered the word.

"No, you lie." Emmett shook his head. "You can't do that. Once they're in the—"

"And Wardens don't have mates, right?" Zeke countered. The truth rang in that single word from his partner. "What else did the five families do?"

He saw Dylan's flinch and cursed himself for causing it, but there was no hiding the truth.

"You think…" Levy murmured.

"There were four wolves. Three shifted and one male reading from an old book. If I had to guess, it's the Clerinell family Grimoire, though they're pretty tight with the Sarvis family, so it could have been theirs. It was hard to tell."

"And how," Levy's voice was soft, but Zeke recognized the underlying warning in his tone, "do you know so much about their Grimoires?"

Zeke's wolf rushed forward, ready to defend their partner. His magic joined the animal, prepared to burst into action the moment it was needed. The gathered males wouldn't be able to sense that he rode the edge of violence, but Dylan knew him. The man shot him a cautioning look, but Zeke didn't give a damn. He'd stood by Dylan for too long to have a Ruling Warden destroy his friend.

Dylan drew air into his lungs and Zeke leaned forward, slowly placing his elbows on his knees. He let his hands hang between his thighs. It seemed like a relaxed pose, but Zeke's wolf went to work as he attempted to appear uncaring.

His skin prickled, the animal lurking beneath the surface. His pores stung with the anticipation of fur bursting from within. His nails ached, the human's weakness ready to be replaced by a wolf's weapons. It would take a single breath to release the beast and magic.

Dylan's voice was strong when he answered the Ruling Warden's question, but he knew his partner fought to suppress his fear. That feeling, that scent, was something they'd trained to eradicate. They succeeded. "I know so much because I once belonged to the

Clerinell family. And," Dylan swallowed and Zeke's wolf snarled at being held back. They should tackle their partner before he could reveal the truth and open himself up for attack. "And the male reading from the Grimoire was Maxim Clerinell. My brother."

*

Dylan closed his eyes, refusing to see the hatred and disgust on their faces. He wasn't proud of his family connections. It was why, after he was kicked out of the house at thirteen and taken in by Zeke's family, he changed his name. The Roberts family had no connection to the five families. They were working class and never batted an eye when Dylan was dragged home by his best friend and just never left.

It hadn't taken much convincing to get his father to approve Dylan's adoption and Zeke's parents had taken Dylan's choice of name in stride. No, Mrs. Roberts merely gave him a tight hug, a kiss on the head and murmured that it was his decision.

So, for seventeen years, he'd been Dylan Clarke. The boy with no past.

Now he was Dylan Clarke. The son of Walter Clerinell—one of the men who'd done their best to destroy Emmett, Levy, and Whitney. He was also the brother of Maxim Clerinell—the wolf who'd tried to kidnap Lorelei mid-teleport.

Whitney and Dylan would have been there as well, but he had a feeling that Maxim was after Lorelei. His brother's focus, his intent gaze, was on the prone woman and not on Dylan or Whitney.

No, Maxim wanted his mate.

His brother didn't know he'd never get his paws on her.

"Excuse me?" Madden's voice was soft, the words hardly above a whisper, but he sensed the wolf's suppressed violence.

"I am Dylan Clerinell. My brother Maxim attempted to tear Whitney, Lorelei, and me from the void. He almost succeeded. I had to pull on Lorelei's power to get us out. Combined with Whitney's efforts, we were able to break free." He refused to let the words tremble as he pushed them forward. Yes, he was a Clerinell, but he was Dylan Clarke, adopted son of the Roberts clan.

Levy growled. "Why didn't she say anything? Why didn't *you*?"

He closed his eyes and thought back to the adrenaline filled fight. "I don't think she remembers. She was consumed by magic. I mean… I couldn't even see the color of her eyes. She was white. It wasn't a glow, it was…" He shook his head. "God damn, she was pure magic. And I…"

Maybe he was a pussy after all.

"And I used Lorelei." He sighed. "But the women's lives were more important to me than—"

"Than telling us that the threat hit damn close to home," Madden snarled at him and Dylan didn't have anything to say to that.

Apparently Zeke did because he shot to his feet and bared his teeth at the Ruling Alpha. The man always was a hothead. Especially when it came to defending Dylan. His friend still hadn't realized Dylan wasn't a battered and beaten kid any longer.

"What? So you can do what you're doing now? You forget that he fucking saved your mate's sister, asshole." That was Zeke, the king of discretion.

Levy jumped into the verbal fray. "Whitney wouldn't have been in danger if—"

Zeke bared a fang. "Fuck you, you know she would have. She was transporting them. If it wasn't Dylan's brother, it would have been some other wolf from the five families. Everyone knows the wolf who kidnapped Rebecca last night was from the Dannel family. That clan is powerful, but they breed idiots. So, that was one of five. How hard is it to figure out the other four are here and they're pissed?"

"Maybe he's in on it," Levy shot back. "Maybe they were waiting—"

Dylan didn't think of the consequences or what it would mean for him to react to those words. He just *did.* In one monstrous leap, he went after Levy. Somewhere in the back of his mind, he knew the wolf was one of the Ruling Wardens. Dylan understood Levy could destroy him without thought.

But that didn't stop him.

His claws burst forward first, human hands giving way to wolfen paws in an instant. His face slowly followed, the bones snapping and reshaping as he flew through the air. The shift after they emerged from the void had weakened him, but he still had enough strength to take the Warden down. They tumbled to the ground in a knot of fang, claw, and magic.

Levy hadn't expected the attack and Dylan knew why. It was suicide to go after a Ruling Warden. Not because it was a death offense. Merely because the Ruling Wardens were the rulers for a reason. They were the strongest.

Dylan grunted when his back struck the carpet, Levy atop him, and he rolled until he straddled the Warden. He didn't punch, didn't strike or scratch the male. No, he simply wrapped on claw tipped hand around the wolf's throat and then pressed the other to Levy's forehead.

"Bear witness," he hissed the words, his wolf's teeth making speech difficult.

Then he made Levy watch the horrors of seventeen years ago.

No, it wasn't just witnessing. It was experiencing. That was his gift. Through touch, Dylan's thoughts became another's reality. With instruction, with the proper training, he could kill a person.

With fear.

That wasn't his intent now. No, it was merely a replaying of Dylan's history.

Of sharpened nails.

Of wicked blades.

Of evil smiles.

And blood. There had been a lot of blood.

All because he wouldn't remove the obstacles from his father's path. With his dad, obstacles weren't inanimate objects. No, they were wolves. Alphas, Wardens, and even humans who opposed him. The only reason he still lived was that Zeke's uncle was a powerful Warden who was able to heal the damage to Dylan's body all those years ago. Then, days later, when Dylan finally woke, he clung to Mrs. Roberts. He attached himself to her side with tears dripping from his lashes.

Twenty-four hours later he was her son. Two weeks after that, he was Dylan Clarke.

Since that day, he hadn't delved deeply into himself to bring those powers forward.

Levy jerked from Dylan's touch, wrenching his head from Dylan's grasp with a harsh gasp. Yellow eyes met Dylan's and he didn't flinch beneath their weight. Now it was up to the Warden if he continued to live. He had his reasons to attack Levy in such a way, but that didn't erase what he'd done.

Dylan dimly heard rough shouts and snarls and he slowly realized he hadn't been interrupted. No one had pulled him from the Ruling Warden. He diverted his gaze, hunting for the reason why he'd been able to complete the task. And he found it. Found it in Lorelei, clinging to Zeke, and glowing brighter than the sun. A shimmering ball encircled them, covering him and Levy in a bubble of… protection.

Damn, his mate was strong. He'd never met a female so fierce and determined.

Now done, he rolled from Levy and waited for the wolf's reaction. How long would it take the Warden to kill him? One minute? Two? He hoped it was less rather than more.

Levy stood and the moment two feet separated them, the aura of protection released the Ruling Warden and covered Dylan alone. Glares were shot his way, Emmett narrowing his eyes and curling his lip while the Ruling Alphas exposed their fangs. He finally noticed that others were near. More guards and a few additional Wardens lingered. As did… the Wickhams and Rebecca and Lorelei.

Everyone had to see it all, of course.

Thankfully, it seemed Scarlet, Gabriella, and Whitney were on his side. As were Rebecca and Lorelei.

Dylan's mate remained in the safety of Zeke's arms, but the other four were spitting mad. He did not envy their mates.

Yells, shouts, and even screeches that made him wince, filled the air. All centered around the same complaint. How *dare* Dylan attack Levy?

It wasn't until Levy placed two fingers in his mouth and blew a harsh whistle that it quieted. Everyone fell silent, wolf and human alike.

"Thank you." Levy straightened his shirt. "Dylan didn't have anything to do with what happened today. He has no contact with the five families." Levy met Dylan's gaze. "And we'll leave it at that."

Emmett stepped toward Dylan. "How can you say that? He almost—"

"He," Levy's voice was firm and low, "is not involved."

The Ruling Wardens then stared at each other and Emmett spoke. "You will stake our mate's life on that."

"Yes." The one word was said without hesitation.

Dylan got a glare, but Emmett jerked his head in a sharp nod. "Fine."

Fine? Dylan certainly hoped so, but he didn't have much faith that he spoke the truth. They still had his brother out there somewhere with the three other wolves.

He knew the Dannel wolf died last night. Assuming one representative from each of the five meant he'd been faced with the remaining four. Now, they just had to be found before they located Paisley since he'd be *damned* if the quartet got another chance at his mate. He met Zeke's gaze. Their mate.

He let his attention drift to her, to her glowing body enfolded in his partner's arms. She trembled with the weight of her magic, her skin pulsing with light, and the hazel of her irises was almost completely hidden by the glow.

Staring at his tiny, lusciously curved mate, he had only one thought. Well, two, but the first went along with the second. "What now?"

Dylan hoped someone would say, "Mate with Lorelei."

He was not that lucky.

Keller replied to his question. "Now we develop a plan. The remaining four will be located." The Ruling Alpha's gaze encompassed the room, and a sliver of fear crept into Dylan's blood. The wolf didn't have magic, but when that much dominance clung to a male's skin… it wasn't needed. "And then they will be killed."

Well, maybe delaying the mating a little while wasn't so bad. He'd at least get to kill something.

# Chapter Five

Lorelei was pretty sure her mates—mates? weird—were pouting because they didn't get to kill someone.

On one hand, she was sad for them. She'd been unconscious when the attempted kidnapping had gone down, but the wolves did try to take her and Whitney…

Plus, those werewolves were also after Paisley.

So, yeah, she was wishing the men—her men—got to tear those four guys into very small pieces. On the other hand, that new part of her craved their presence. No, not just their presence. Their touch. She wanted them to touch her. All over. All of the touching of her body.

Lorelei sat sandwiched between the two men, the three crowded on the small couch. With Zeke to her left and Dylan to her right, safety and comfort surrounded her. It enveloped her even as they all spoke of the best way to hunt and kill their opponents.

She only vaguely heard. Exhaustion and fatigue still dogged her, and her body would love nothing more than fall into bed in a heap. A heap that would also contain Dylan and Zeke. The overwhelming thrum of energy she'd felt only hours ago was settled into a rumbling idle. Whitney assured her it'd ease further now that the "Big Blow Up of Doom" was over. Her magic would react to emotion at this point and after they mated, it'd reduce even more.

*Then* she'd be able to gain full control of her power.

She leaned her head against Dylan's shoulder, sensing his need for a snuggle even if he wouldn't voice the words. While she pressed against one mate, she grasped Zeke's arm with her free hand, unwilling to lose the connection to either man. When she sighed in relief, she sensed some of their tension ease as well. It was as if they remained anxious and on edge as long as she did.

Murmured voices filled the air, the occasional snarl or growl punctuating words, but for the most part it stayed civil. Even the women, her cousins and sister, kept their frustrations and anger contained. If the Wickhams were anything like the Twynhams, it was a miracle they hadn't ripped anyone's head off. Metaphorically speaking.

They didn't actually decapitate people. Then again…

"Miles and Holden will continue their search for Paisley, while we dispatch Alpha and Warden Pairs to nearby hotels, but there is still one issue at hand." Lorelei sensed the unease in Keller's tone. The man was *the* Ruling Alpha. What had him scared?

"And we said no." Zeke's words were calm, but a new tension had his muscles tightening.

"Don't you think she should get a choice?" Madden countered.

"Not when it means one of you touching her. The answer is no." Dylan's voice was smooth as ice.

"It's the only way. Carson and Aidan already said no. You three aren't mated yet. That means she can choose for herself," Keller volleyed.

"Carson and Aidan said no to what?" Rebecca pulled away from one of her mates and eased to her feet before spinning on the males. "You said no to what?"

Oh, Lorelei knew *that* tone.

"Baby…" Lorelei was pretty sure that was Aidan. Who knew a bad ass guy could sound so sweet.

Unfortunately for him, Rebecca wasn't falling for it.

She hoped Zeke and Dylan took notes because the Twynhams were alike in some things. Such as men taking choices away from them.

Rather than watch Rebecca get into a verbal fight with her mates, Lorelei got to the real point. She tore her gaze from her sister and focused on Keller. "What do you need us to do?" Twin growls surrounded her, but she wasn't going to be denied. "Zip it, guys."

"Miles and Holden can find people easily when we're limited to ground level. Even a few stories are okay, but we're looking at twenty floors and then there are the basement levels and parking." Keller shook his head.

"They tried to find Paisley after touching Rebecca, but it wasn't enough. They need a blood sample."

Lorelei furrowed her brow. "That's it? And they'll be able to find her then?"

"It's very, very likely. It'll be a deeper connection." Keller nodded.

"Why not let Scarlet donate?" Zeke snarled.

The other Ruling Alpha leaned forward, death written into every feature. "Do you think we could stop her if that's what she wanted? Neither of us would like it, but it's for family and above all, Scarlet values family. If she was a close enough relative to Paisley, she would. But she's not and we have her sisters here."

Dylan tensed as if he'd rise and Lorelei leaned away to grab his wrist. "Wait a minute. Calm down," she murmured before turning her attention back to the Ruling Alphas. "Okay, that's what has everyone's panties in a bunch?" She focused on Carson and Aidan. "And you wouldn't let Rebecca donate? Seriously? It's our *sister*. One asshole has already tried to take Rebecca and another four came after me, Whitney, and Dylan. And you're still saying no?"

Rebecca stepped away from her mates and she almost felt bad for the two wolves when she saw their expressions. The two men looked like their very souls were walking away from them. Then again, wasn't that the truth?

"You…" Rebecca sounded heartbroken and Lorelei pushed up from the couch.

She reached her sister and drew her close, wrapping her arm around Rebecca's shoulders. "Shh, we'll take care of it now." Lorelei glanced at Emmett and Levy. "How do we do this?"

"Lorelei…" Zeke's warning came with a rumbling growl.

"No." She shook her head. "I get the whole wolf possessive thing, but she's my sister. After all of this mess… Rebecca and Paisley are all I have left, Zeke. My parents, my grandmother… they're gone as far as I'm concerned. I don't have a family beyond my sisters. We're all each other has."

Heartbreak filled his gaze and it was as if she saw it shatter. "You have us, Lorelei."

She let her hand drift from Rebecca and padded toward the gorgeous man. She cupped his cheek, ignoring the flash of light that came with the contact. With her free hand, she grasped Dylan and tugged him closer.

"I know, and my sisters don't make what we're building any less. But… she's my little sister, Zeke, and God knows what they're doing to her. I don't…" Lorelei's heart clenched. "I don't think she's merely hiding. I think there's something wrong. She's in trouble. I feel it. Let me do this."

Lorelei met his yellow-eyed gaze, sinking into his focus and praying that he sensed her need.

Emmett cleared his throat, drawing everyone's attention, but she didn't let her focus stray from Zeke. "It's not just a matter of sticking a needle in a vein, here. The reason your mates object isn't because of any pain you endure, it's the *way* the blood is drawn." He sighed. "And then there's what happens *after*."

Zeke's orbs flared bright and she noticed a similar light coming from Dylan.

"How do they get it?" Lorelei called to the Warden. "And what do you mean 'after'?"

"They will have to take your blood from the source."

A snap and crack reached her a single moment before she noticed Zeke's jaw wasn't so human-shaped any longer.

"So, they have to bite me?" Lorelei rubbed her thumb along his reshaped jaw.

"No, a cut is sufficient. They'll lick what comes to the surface."

A rumbling growl came from Dylan and she stroked the inside of his wrist.

"Cut, then lick. Easy enough. So, what's the problem?" It wouldn't be fun, but she'd endure a little pain for her sister. No question.

"In Rebecca's case, her mates would lose it and would try to kill Miles and Holden. Then they'd reclaim her. Of course, there's no telling how long that will take.

They're mated and their wolves would see the Wardens' touch as a challenge." Emmett's explanation was slow and she imagined there was more.

"And in my case?" There had to be a "but" in there somewhere.

"In your case, you're not mated. So while Zeke and Dylan are very possessive, it's not to the extent of Aidan and Carson. You haven't been claimed." Emmett sighed. "If you do this, if you allow Miles and Holden to take your blood, you *will* be mated shortly thereafter. Zeke and Dylan's wolves won't allow anything less than a full binding."

To save her sister, she'd have to sacrifice her life to the two men before her. Everyone spoke as if it was the end of the world. And… she slowly realized it wasn't.

No, not in the slightest. True, she would have preferred more time to get to know the men, but Whitney was right. There was something inside her that screamed to take the two men and make them hers.

Hers.

"You said Rebecca, Carson, and Aidan would go at it and no one knows how long they'd be 'otherwise occupied.' I can see why that'd be a bad thing. Is there a reason I shouldn't mate them right now? Will it take us out of the game for days, too?"

"There isn't a reason. You should be finished with your initial mating rush by morning. With luck, we'll have Paisley in hand by then." A hint of hope filled

Emmett's voice and she sensed Rebecca's rising excitement.

The emotions lurking in her mates' eyes were a mixture of regret, anger, and desperate need. She'd address their worries, their fury at the way this was coming about, later.

Right now…

"Call Miles and Holden to the suite."

*

Zeke wasn't sure whose objection was louder, his or Dylan's. Regardless, they both bellowed the same response.

"No!"

While everyone in the room flinched, Lorelei did not. No, she remained in place, shouldering their displeasure and appearing as if she couldn't care less.

Well, she could "not care" all she wanted because he refused to have another wolf's mouth… A rush of pain and adrenaline skated through his veins, and the wolf leapt forward. His magic was right behind the renewed sensations, and those parts of him were intent on killing Miles and Holden the minute they appeared.

Lorelei sighed and removed her hand from his face. He nearly whimpered. Nearly. He was a little smug that when she did the same with Dylan, his partner whined and Zeke hadn't.

She stared at them both, her jaw clenched tightly and lips pressed together until they formed a pale line on her face. A stubborn twinkle invaded her eyes and he realized he was going to lose this argument. Dammit.

This wasn't how he wanted things to happen. He hadn't wanted their mating to come about because of the need to find her sister. It was supposed to be more. Maybe it wouldn't have been love; it was too soon for that. But he'd hoped for more than biological undeniable need.

He looked over her head and sought out Levy and Emmett. "What *exactly* is going to happen?"

"It's probably best if we all discuss it when Miles and Holden arr—"

"No, I'm asking you. I can't guarantee we won't take them down as soon as they walk through the door if we're kept in the dark." Zeke cracked his neck, rolling his head from side to side as he fought to banish the growing tension. "The wolf needs to know."

Zeke didn't bother telling them that his magic needed the assurance as well. The power pulsing inside them was at their beck and call and yet it wasn't. It had a vague consciousness of its own and was known to react before the Warden realized the danger he faced.

"Zeke, you can't be considering—"

Zeke faced his friend. "Do you want to be the one to tell our mate that we left her sister to be picked off by your brother? Because I sure as hell don't."

"But they'll touch…"

They'll touch what belonged to them. Sure, Dylan loved Zeke's parents and family, and they loved his friend in return, but it wasn't *Dylan's* family. Lorelei was the wolf's chance at having one of his own. *His.*

He placed his hand on Dylan's shoulder and forced the man to face him, sliding his hand up until it wrapped around the back of Dylan's neck. "I know you, D. I know what this is and you need to let it happen."

"You're telling me you're okay with this? That they'll put their teeth to her?" His partner's voice was filled with shock.

Yeah, Zeke was pretty shocked himself. "*Okay* is a stretch." In fact, his wolf howled at the mere idea someone else would dare bare a fang in her presence. "But can you honestly tell me you'd let an innocent woman suffer because our wolves and magic are pissy?" He tugged Dylan toward him, pressing their foreheads together. "We're stronger than this, D. And we're gonna do it because we care for our mate, huh?"

Dylan's eyes closed and Zeke knew he'd won. His friend's next words proved his assumption. "How does it work?"

When his partner pulled away, Zeke let him retreat. The moment space existed between him and Dylan, Lorelei was there, tugging them close to her until she was sandwiched between their bodies. His cock twitched and the wolf discarded anger in favor of interest.

*Soon.* He told his wolf. *Very soon.*

He hated it'd come about this way, but he wouldn't refuse her if she was prepared to accept them.

Levy cleared his throat and everyone's attention was centered on the Ruling Warden. "Ideally, both men would bite her."

Zeke echoed Dylan's rumbling growl. Lorelei stroked them both, her small hands sliding over their arms, but even her touch had difficulties banishing his possessive rage. "No one is putting fang to our mate."

"Okay," Levy huffed. "The other option is to cut into her skin and let them drink there. Regardless, it'll still be deep and painful. I'll call in a Warden pair that will heal her as soon as it's done, but during the actual process," Levy grimaced, "she can't be sedated. The… the agony will have her calling out, even subconsciously, for comfort. Her soul will automatically call to people in her family who are closest. Rebecca and… Paisley. It adds that emotion to her blood and that's what they'll pull on."

The Ruling Warden focused on Lorelei, regret and sadness in his gaze. "I'm sorry, but it's the only way."

His mate turned her head into his chest, burying her face against him. She shuddered once, a hint of her fear reaching his nose, but she nodded her agreement.

"I'll… I'll do it." Her voice trembled and Zeke fought the urge to shift and destroy whatever frightened their mate.

Zeke sensed the same desire from Dylan, and he met his partner's gaze over Lorelei's head. He saw the same conviction, the same anger, and the same possessive light in Dylan's eyes that he felt inside.

Neither liked the idea, but neither would stop it, either.

"And after?" Zeke voiced the question, knowing and hating himself at his excitement and anticipation with the answer.

Emmett's voice was grim. "After… You'll have to hold onto your wolves and magic long enough for them to heal her. Once that's done, we'll leave you three alone. There's a set of rooms on the other side of the suite that we'll use for the transfer and healing. Then we'll all remain on this side. By tomorrow morning you should be… done."

Done. A pretty way to dress up their—essentially forced—mating.

Zeke shook his head. For the last year, as he'd dreamed of finding a mate, he hadn't anticipated it'd come about this way. He'd imagined… coaxing and sweet words and… more than a fuck fueled by other males touching their mate.

"How long until they get here?" Lorelei's voice was soft.

"We'll call them now. It shouldn't be more than ten or fifteen minutes, depending on where they are in the building," Levy spoke softly.

"Okay, if it's okay with you guys, I'd like to go to the room and talk to Zeke and Dylan alone." She sounded unsure and embarrassed and those were two emotions she should never experience. Not with them.

"Of course." Levy nodded and stepped back. "This way."

Zeke wasn't sure if she'd go through with it, if she'd take the first step to follow the Ruling Warden. But she did. She put one foot in front of the other and padded across the carpet. The room remained quiet, completely silent, save the shuffle of her bare feet and the brush of their shoes on the floor.

As they walked past Rebecca, the woman reached for their mate, stopping her sister's progress. Rebecca hauled Lorelei into her arms. "I love you. More than the moon."

"I love you more than the moon and the stars," Lorelei whispered and he realized it was a small ritual between the two sisters. Something beautiful shared by women who meant the world to each other.

Zeke prayed they'd someday have something similar.

"They'll find her, right, Lor?" Rebecca sounded so small and broken. Nothing like the vivacious woman who had given her mates a hard time.

Lorelei pressed a kiss to Rebecca's cheek. "Of course. They'll be too afraid of Zeke and Dylan to fail." They exchanged a quick hug and then Lorelei stepped back. "I'll see you tomorrow, huh? All freshly mated?"

At her sister's nod, Lorelei continued on her path, following Levy across the suite, past little sitting areas and other rooms until they came to a set of double doors.

Lorelei was the first to step into the room and Zeke and Dylan were on her heels. She paused by the bed, staring at the smooth surface for a moment before she stroked the blanket.

"Not here." She turned her attention to a far corner and Zeke realized a few chairs surrounded a low table. "There." She nodded. "Yeah, there. And… I need a couple of minutes alone with the guys. We'll open the door when we're ready."

Levy nodded and quietly retreated as their mate made her way to the cushioned seat.

When she settled onto the seat, Zeke dragged another chair over to her while Dylan did the same. They sat and stared at her, waiting to find out why she'd asked for time alone before…

"So, we're gonna be mated." She flashed a rueful grin. "I'm okay with it, but I didn't even ask… Is-is this something you two want?"

Zeke didn't think, didn't even hesitate. No, he acted on instinct alone. One moment she sat in the chair beside him and the next she was on his lap. He definitely didn't ask for permission when he sealed his lips to hers. She stiffened against him, but when he traced the seam of her lips with his tongue, she immediately relaxed into his kiss.

Lorelei opened for him, allowing him to drink from her mouth and absorb her sweet flavors. She was sex and sin and so damned delicious. He wasn't sure he'd ever get enough of her. His cock throbbed with the need to have her, to take her and make her his.

Theirs.

She gripped his shoulders, fingernails digging into his flesh. Her tongue tangled with his, tasting him as he explored her. When she moaned against his mouth, he did the same, his groan slowly transforming into a growl of need.

God damn. He'd never get enough of her.

Lorelei's arousal perfumed the air, the heady musk filling his nose, and he distantly heard his partner snarl. Yeah, Dylan wanted Lorelei as much as he did and it wasn't fair to keep their mate all to himself.

Just one more taste…

He suckled her tongue and gathered more of her flavors. When she wiggled her hips against him, he groaned, his cock pulsing and hardening further, demanding he sink into her wet heat.

Soon. God, he hoped it'd be soon.

Right after… His mind shied from the pending truth. He would savor their kiss and pray it got him through the coming confrontation.

When his friend began a rolling rumble, he knew his time was at an end.

Zeke pulled from Lorelei's lips, ignoring her whimpering protest. He cupped her cheek and forced her to meet his gaze. "Your other mate needs you, baby."

Her dilated eyes widened and then a flash of need filled her expression. She turned on his lap until she faced Dylan and he fought the urge to moan. His partner deserved her full attention now. They'd both get their fill of Lorelei after all was said and done.

"Dylan? Do you—"

*

Dylan didn't let her finish her question. His cock was rock hard and ready to burst through his slacks. There was no room for nice and sweet and seductive. No, he was pure need and animalistic desire. His wolf rode him, his magic pushing past the animal to reach Lorelei.

His. His. And his again.

He met Zeke's gaze for a brief moment.

No, theirs. He had to remember that even as the wolf howled that he should race away with her.

He reached for Lorelei and hauled her to him, adopting a position similar to the one she'd shared with Zeke. Across his lap, her lush body was at his mercy. Her berry colored lips swollen from his partner's kisses tempted him, but it was the seductive scent of her arousal that called to him more. It coated her skin, every inch of her creamy flesh trembled with her need.

Dylan captured her lips much like Zeke, but that's where the similarities ended. Zeke, with his carefree attitude, was passionate, but not like Dylan.

He didn't hold Dylan's history, his anger, his power.

He didn't have the things that made Dylan dangerous.

Teeth scraped and bit her lips, nibbling and sucking on the small bits of flesh when his tongue wasn't deep in her mouth.

Lorelei squirmed and moaned against him and he felt her pebbled nipples hard against his chest. Answering her soft plea, he cupped one mound, squeezing and kneading. It was easy to capture one nipple between thumb and forefinger. Easy to pluck the nub and pinch it ever so slightly.

A gasp hinted at the sting he caused and the shudder told him she enjoyed the small bite. Oh, his sweet, sexy mate liked a little brush of pain.

He was happy to give her whatever she desired.

He sucked on her tongue in time with his naughty attentions to her breast, drawing her deeper into his sensuous spell. Her moans and groans warred with his own.

Did he want to mate her? Yes. *Yes.*

There was no question and he hoped she didn't cling to it any longer.

Lorelei rocked her hips, wiggling and squirming, drawing his attention to her ass. And what lay hidden between her thighs.

It would take no time to free himself, tear her shorts away and sink into her heat. No time at all…

But that meant he'd mate her. Mate her before they performed the ritual to find Paisley and she'd never forgive him if his actions prevented that.

So, he eased their kiss, slowed his caresses and lowered his hand to her hip as he withdrew from her lips. She panted, bathing him with the moist air of her heavy breathing, and collapsed against his chest. She rested her head on his shoulder, snuggling close.

He met his partner's gaze, noting that he rode the edge of control as well. They needed to get this done so they could claim their mate.

"Lorelei," he murmured, and she released a questioning whimper. "I don't like the way this came about. I don't like that you're being forced to accept this mating because we won't be able to control ourselves. But do not, for a second, think we don't want this. I would have claimed you the moment we touched if you'd been willing."

"And if I hadn't been a human-sized nightlight," she drawled.

"That too." He grinned.

Lorelei buried her face against his neck and her words were hardly more than a mumble. "I don't want you two to feel trapped."

Dylan's "never" was echoed by Zeke's "fuck that."

Then his partner was there, kneeling, his hands stroking their mate. "Baby, D's right. If it wasn't for the fact we have to take you together, I would have laid you out on the damned hallway floor and tasted every inch of your skin. I would have put my mark on you and made sure every male that came into contact with you knew you were mine."

Dylan rubbed his cheek on the top of her head, transferring his scent to her. Those Wardens needed to know she *was* theirs even without the bite. "You're ours, sweet. Ours and no one else's. Don't think we're being forced or we're trapped. If anything, we know we're moving fast. We know it, but are selfish enough not to care because in the end… it means you're ours."

Okay, he admitted that made him sound like a dick. Didn't mean he'd take it back though. He'd been missing having a family and now it was within his grasp. He was not above taking advantage of the situation.

"Okay," she whispered and tilted her head back to meet his gaze. "Okay." Then she focused on Zeke. "Tell Levy we're ready."

*

Lorelei prayed she was ready. Deep gouges and blood drinking did not sound like an enjoyable experience. At all. She was excited about the mating though. Belonging to them—them belonging to her—sounded like heaven. They were strong and gorgeous and… they made her feel beautiful.

The soft click of the bedroom door's knob disengaging reached her and then low murmurs followed in its wake.

Ready. She was ready. Right.

The sound of several people entering the suite filled her ears and she tensed, knowing what was to come. They'd surround her, cut her, drink her blood and then heal her.

*Then* she'd mate with Zeke and Dylan.

Ouch. Ew. Fix. Boom-bang.

Right.

Dylan must have sensed her unease because then he was stroking her, hand sliding over her arm and then fingers entwining with hers. "We'll be right here. The moment they're done, we'll have you and from now on, nothing will ever hurt you again. I swear it."

"*We* swear it." Zeke loomed over them, deep frown in place.

Lorelei nodded. "Okay." She took a deep breath and released it slowly. "Okay, let's do this."

Dylan shifted as if to rise and she clung to him.

"What are you doing?" She practically screeched the words but didn't care.

"We'll be touching your shoulders, but Emmett and Levy have to keep us from going after the Wardens who have to touch you." He pressed a firm kiss to her lips. "Otherwise, we'd kill them."

Wow. Okay then. "Alright." She eased from his lap and took his place in the chair, remaining tense until she had the heavy weight of their hands on her shoulders. "I'm really ready now."

It wasn't long before they *were* doing it.

Two men who introduced themselves as Miles and Holden slowly eased past her mates and came to stand on either side of her. They kept their distance and it wasn't until Zeke and Dylan tensed that she realized why. The Ruling Wardens finally restrained them.

"Miss Twynham? Are you ready?" The man on her right spoke low. Holden. He was Holden.

Lorelei closed her eyes, unwilling to see what would come, and nodded.

Then she simply felt. She noted the roughness of Holden's fingers while Miles' were smooth. Miles' touch was firm and sure, while Holden's was gentler. They were opposites and yet, they seemed perfect for each other.

That new part of her bristled at their stroke, but she begged it to stay back. She couldn't find Paisley without the two men. Family seemed to be something the magic in her understood and it retreated.

They murmured words she didn't understand, their thumbs pressed against her pulse point as they spoke. It had to be some sort of spell, something that would help them, and she took a deep breath, determined to remain passive as they worked.

The press of cool metal to her skin told her what was to come. She fought to push the impending pain from her mind and keep it at bay. Screaming would only enrage her mates further, and that couldn't happen. She had to endure. She had to get through this.

That cold was immediately followed by pain. No, agony. The blades sliced into her skin, digging deeply and she arched her back, battled the anguish that filled her veins. It pulsed and pounded in time with her heart and still she remained silent. She allowed a harsh inhale, but nothing else. She tilted her head back, eyes squeezed shut against the room as she demanded her body to listen to her.

It didn't give a fuck. No, it allowed her to remain quiet, but her magic—her power—told her to take a flying leap. It screamed and battered her, raging against the pain she endured. Warmth enveloped her and she knew it was that part of her pushing past her control.

Dammit.

But it wasn't attacking the men. No, it had a singular purpose.

It didn't attack. It fed. It fed them her thoughts, her feelings, her… connection to Paisley.

Yes, her soul called out to her younger sister, and the magic inside her made sure the two Wardens had exactly what they needed to hunt her down.

Distantly, she accepted that Paisley was with Dylan's brother. With him and… not in the hotel.

No, she was—

The two men drew harder on her wounds, sucking more blood from her body and she realized… they liked it. They wanted more.

Her power was no longer helpful. No, it was a hindrance. It drew them like bees to honey and they craved just one more drop.

No.

That power, her strength, was for her mates alone.

Lorelei didn't even have to ask for assistance from that piece of her. No, it recognized what the Wardens were doing, and it was a mere thought that had the two wolves flying from her body. With the pain still thrumming through her veins, she lowered her head and watched as the men were propelled across the room, their backs colliding with the wall and sending drywall dust raining down. Gasps surrounded her, but she didn't have time to worry about everyone's response. Not when blood flowed freely.

"Heal me," she thought she whispered, she was pretty sure she tried, but the air seemed to tremble and shake with the strength of her voice. The walls rumbled with the force.

Two men rushed forward, eyes wide, hands glowing as they approached. Her magic tasted the males, slid through their bodies and finally let them approach. That part of her weighed and examined them, still fighting to protect her. An invisible guard dog. Lorelei huffed a small chuckle and she noticed the way everyone shuffled a step. She should be quiet.

The Wardens stopped just short of touching her, their gazes meeting hers for a moment and she nodded. She'd like to *not* bleed to death.

The tingle and warmth of her knitting flesh and skin soothed her power, sent it sliding to the back of her mind with a soft sigh. It relaxed, allowing Lorelei to breathe normally once again, and the moment the pain receded fully, she jerked from the Wardens' touch. She appreciated their help, but she couldn't stand anyone else's hands on her. Or mouths. She shuddered, remembering their desire for her blood.

"Get out. Thank you, but everyone out." This time her words *were* a whisper, but it was as if she'd threatened their lives. The healing Wardens reached for Miles and Holden, helping them to their feet, and she had a few other things to say. "They don't search alone. They don't go anywhere near Paisley alone."

"It's best if—" Miles was the first to object.

"I felt your emotions. Every. Single. One. You won't go near her alone." She shook her head.

"That was a mistake." Holden grimaced. "We're sorry."

"What did they do?" Dylan's low question was much calmer than Zeke's snarl. Though she knew, of the two men, it was Dylan she'd have to worry about.

When both men paled and swallowed hard, she knew they were aware of the size of their mistake.

"We'll discuss it after they find Paisley." She tilted her head back to meet first Zeke's gaze and then Dylan's. "And after we mate." She refocused on the two chagrinned males. "Leave. You have enough to find her. You know where to start looking."

Both men nodded and eased past them, giving their fivesome a wide berth. She knew Emmett and Levy were still near. Otherwise her mates would have gone after the two Wardens.

Lorelei pushed to her feet, swaying slightly as she stood. Damn. The pain was gone, but she was the tiniest bit lightheaded. She shook her head, brushing off the feeling and finally looked to the four men. Zeke and Dylan's faces were peppered with gray fur, their cheeks more pronounced and fangs pressed against their lower lips.

"You can let them go now." She focused on Emmett and Levy. "I'll be safe with Dylan and Zeke."

And she realized she truly would. No matter what, she would be safe with Zeke and Dylan. They were, after all, her mates.

# CHAPTER SIX

Zeke held onto his control by a thread and he knew his partner was just as stressed by the events that'd unfolded before them.

Lorelei had to use her magic to repel the two Wardens and he hadn't missed the catch in her voice when she demanded Miles and Holden be monitored. Everything in him commanded he chase the two wolves down and cut their throats for upsetting her.

Excessive? Probably.

Necessary? Absolutely.

As if reading his thoughts, she reached up and patted his hand with her trembling palm. "Hush, I'm fine."

It was then he realized he was growling and he forced the wolf to back off. No sense in snarling now. Not when the men were gone and hunting for Paisley.

That left him with Dylan and Lorelei.

His partner and his mate. A mate he was more than ready to claim.

His wolf howled in anticipation while his skin buzzed with his power, the energy skating over his flesh as it prepared to twine and sink into his mate. His cock throbbed and pulsed, aching to be free but he held onto his control. Barely. They'd warned her of their desires—that after others put their mouths on her, Zeke and Dylan would need to replace their scent. Replace it and change it with their own bites.

Everyone needed to know she was claimed.

"You're not fine." Dylan did growl and he shot his friend a harsh look. Getting angry with her for helping her sister would not help things along.

"I am." She tilted her head back, gaze shifting from Dylan to Zeke and back again. "I'd be better if my mates fulfilled their promise."

Zeke eased around the chair and perched on the wide arm, knowing it'd easily take his weight. All of the furniture in the hotel was made for werewolves—solid and sturdy.

"What promise is that, baby?" Zeke brushed strands of hair away from her eyes.

"You know," she whispered, her pale face flushing pink.

"Oh, I think you do." Dylan mirrored Zeke's position. "Tell us, sweet."

She licked her lips, and his dick twitched. He wanted to follow that pink tongue and lap at her tastes. Even more, he wanted her tracing his shaft before suckling the head of his cock.

Damn.

"I want…" Her attention bounced between them. "I want to be your mate. You said you'd be out of control, but it doesn't seem—"

Zeke couldn't have stopped himself had he tried. Not when worry and disappointment filled the air. Her worry and disappointment. His attempt at control made her doubt them.

That was unacceptable.

Zeke swooped in and captured her lips, cupping her face and tilting her head as he desired. The small twist gave him deeper access, allowed him to thrust his tongue deep and dominate their meeting. He wanted to brand her with his mouth, take control and show her who she belonged to.

She moaned and clutched his shoulders, small nails digging into his flesh, but not piercing his skin. When he sucked on her tongue, she whined anew, pushing closer to him and pulling him toward her. Her arousal replaced her unease and he drew in the heady scent of her need. Sweet and musky and he couldn't wait to taste her. She would be so delicious, flowing over his tongue with each orgasm. She'd come at least a dozen times before the night was through.

Maybe two.

Something else reached his nose, something other than her desire and the hints of Dylan's aching desperation for Lorelei.

It was them. *Them* on her skin and it reminded him of the mouths that'd touched her so recently.

Zeke pulled from the kiss, tearing his mouth away as his wolf rushed forward. His teeth elongated and sharpened, ready to put his mouth to her skin. It wanted to bite her, replace the marks that'd been left.

He tugged her arms from around his neck and stared at the wounds. No, there was no physical reminder of the spell. Her skin was unmarred and part of him relaxed at that fact. But blood still coated her. The wolves had been tossed from her in a blinding rush of power, leaving her to bleed freely for several moments before the healing Wardens were able to repair the damage.

That left remnants of the injuries evident against her paleness. There were also invisible signs of another's touch.

The disgusting hint of Miles and Holden coated her as well.

"We gotta get you in the shower." Zeke's words were hardly audible to himself and he prayed Lorelei understood.

"Z?" Dylan furrowed his brow.

"She smells like them, D. We'll claim her, but…" He focused on Lorelei. "I need their scent off you."

Lorelei nodded, giving him a small smile. "If you'll carry me, we can do whatever you want."

Dylan chuckled. "Don't give us a blanket offer like that, sweet. Because we'll take you up on it."

Her smile turned wicked. "I trust you to do your worst. Or best."

His partner shook his head. "Help her and I'll get the water started." Dylan stroked her cheek. "We'll get you clean and then we'll get you dirty again."

"Sounds like a plan." This time Lorelei winked.

Yes, it sounded like a very, very good plan.

Zeke stood and reached for Lorelei, helping her stand. The moment she was vertical, he swept her into his arms, enjoying the feel of her curves against his body. She sighed and placed her head against his shoulder and arm across his chest. She snuggled in and he nuzzled the top of her head. That part of her was pure Lorelei. The two Wardens were never near her hair and he relished the heavenly scent of her. Those flavors served two purposes: it let his wolf forget about the intruding males while also urging him to claim her. Now. Right this second she needed to belong to them before anyone could take her from them.

The word repeated in his mind with every step.

*Now. Now. Now…*

The splatter of water on tile reached him, the sounds vibrating the air and telling him that Dylan had done as they'd planned. The cool liquid was now warming for them.

Them. If Lorelei thought they'd leave her alone, she was in for a big surprise. Now that anger was leaving him, overwhelming need was sliding into its place. The wolf scratched and scraped at Zeke's skin, demanding he dispense with the sweet words and soft touches.

*Now. Now. Now…*

The heat of the shower reached out to them the moment he and Lorelei crossed the threshold. Crossed it and were met with a bare-chested Dylan. The man's pants were tented, telling him that his friend was in the same shape as Zeke. At least he wasn't the only one hurting.

Dylan approached and brushed his lips over Lorelei's mouth, returning to deepen their kiss for a moment before he backed away. "Let's get you undressed, sweet. Can't wait to peel away all these layers and taste your skin." His partner kissed her again. "And that delicious pussy. You've been teasing us with that scent and I want to lap you up."

Lorelei shuddered and Zeke smiled. It seemed their sexy mate got off on a little dirty talk as well. If she enjoyed hearing about everything they wanted to do to her, he was more than happy to share.

"C'mon, baby. Let's get you stripped and into the shower," he murmured, and padded to the counter.

After gently placing her on the counter, he reached for the buttons on her shirt. A flush turned her pale skin pink and he sensed her embarrassment.

One button gave way to two, which gave way to three and four, exposing more of her lush body with each movement.

"Damn," he sucked in a harsh breath and fought off his own release. "You're so fucking beautiful. Look at these pretties." He undid a few more fasteners and then her lace covered breasts were bared to him. "Do you see how hard her little nipples are, D?"

Zeke reached into her shirt, cupping the mounds and squeezing gently. Her nips were firm against his palms and he shifted his touch to lightly pinch the nubs. At her moan, he knew his little mate enjoyed that tiny bite.

"See how much she wants this, D."

"Damn, sweet." Dylan's voice was husky.

"Please?" she whimpered.

"She wants more, Z. Give our mate what she wants." With Dylan's words, Lorelei shuddered anew.

"Gladly." Zeke grinned. "What do you want, baby? Do you want me to suck these nipples, strip you bare and eat that pussy?"

Another whimper and she finally spoke. "Wanna see you both. Want you to touch me. Want to touch you."

"Oh, we're always happy to do that." Zeke got back to her buttons. "D, finish stripping for our mate while I get my taste."

He noted his friend's movements and the fact that Dylan was putting on a show for Lorelei. While his partner gave her visual stimulation, Zeke went for a more physical approach. He finally parted her shirt, brushing the sides aside giving him full view of her.

"Damn, baby," he whispered and reached for her. It was easy work to divest her of her bra, the silk and lace falling away to reveal the pale globes.

Zeke let his attention drift to her face, and he was floored by the trust and need written in her features. "We're gonna take care of you so good, baby."

It was a promise to both her and himself.

He didn't hesitate to love on her breasts. He licked and nipped, enjoying each sound that escaped her mouth. When he sucked hard, she rocked her hips as if searching for more stimulation. She'd get plenty and hopefully sooner rather than later. Especially considering his cock was ready to burst.

He nibbled the nub and he smiled when she fisted his strands, holding him steady while she arched closer. Yes, their mate was a sensual, sexy woman.

Zeke stroked her as he continued worshipping the mounds. He petted her back, slid over her sides and finally reached for the button of her shorts. He flicked the button and lowered the zipper in a single move.

He'd accept any objection she voiced, but he wanted to strip her before she thought too much.

He released her nipple with a soft pop and met her gaze. "Lift those hips, baby. Let me get rid of your shorts and then we'll make you feel so good. Make you scream."

Lorelei nibbled on her lower lip and did as he asked, letting him tug the material past her hips and down her legs.

"Wanna see you, too," she whispered, her attention bouncing between him and Dylan.

"On one condition." Her eyebrows raised in question. "I get my turn to eat this pussy before the night is through."

Her nod was quick and immediate, her hair brushing forward and sliding over the mounds of her breast. Damn. He couldn't wait to fist those strands as she sucked his cock.

Baby steps. Slow. He had to remind himself that they couldn't do everything in round one. Maybe round two.

"Dylan? Why don't you taste our sweet mate while I strip for her?" Zeke stepped back and gave his now nude partner room so he could kneel between Lorelei's spread thighs.

Fuck, those short brown curls glistened with her arousal. Her pussy practically screamed to be licked and tasted. Maybe he should haul Dylan away from her so he could get the first taste. Zeke closed his eyes and growled at himself. There would be plenty of years ahead of him.

Instead of staring at his partner push his tongue between her sex lips, he reached back and grabbed the fabric of his shirt. One long tug had the material sliding up and over his shoulders until he was free. The steamy air moistened his chest and he didn't miss the way Lorelei's breath caught.

Because she saw him. Not because of Dylan's ministrations, but him and him alone.

He could live with that.

*

Lorelei was gonna die. Between her mates being naked and the sexual promise in their eyes… Yup, deader than dead. With any luck, she'd come a time or ten before all was said and done.

Dylan knelt between her thighs, his wide shoulders forcing her legs even wider as he made room for himself. Yes, his shoulders were wide, his chest was strong and those abs were solid and carved. He was a gorgeous package of strength, and she sensed an inner softness in him that she didn't think he showed many people.

She hoped she'd someday be one of those people.

When Zeke tore his shirt from his body, she nearly swallowed her tongue. Yes, they were both gorgeous, but in different ways, and she ached to discover them.

Zeke stroked his chest, running his hand down his body and then toyed with the button of his jeans.

"See something you like?" Dylan's warm breath fanned her pussy and she moaned, anxious for him to touch her, stroke her. He needed to do something.

"You. You and Zeke." She figured honesty was the best policy. "You're both so gorgeous."

She didn't add on, "and I'm not." No, she swallowed the words, but he must have read her feelings because he narrowed his eyes.

"You're the gorgeous one, Lorelei. Gorgeous and lush and beautiful and sexy as fuck." Dylan's hoarse words touched something inside her and she nodded in agreement.

"You know what else is pretty?"

Lorelei shook her head.

"This pussy."

With that, he showed her how pretty.

Dylan parted her lower lips with his fingers and pressed his mouth to her. There was no teasing build up or gentle caresses. No, he mastered her with the first press of his lips to her body.

His tongue lapped at her clit, licking and tasting her. He sucked and flicked her clit, tormenting her and she sobbed. Unable to stop herself, she fisted his strands, tightening her hand to hold him in place. Her hips moved of their own volition, gently rocking against his talented tongue.

"Dylan…" she whispered his name as a plea for more.

"Does that feel good, baby?" Zeke's words were a husky murmur and she opened her eyes to stare at him.

Hell, she hadn't even realized she'd closed them. But she had and when she gave Zeke her attention, she found him leaning against the counter beside her. His yellowed eyes were trained on Dylan between her thighs, but his hand… One hand wrapped around his cock, slowly stroking himself with gentle movements.

"Does his tongue feel good on your little clit?" he asked her again and she nodded, turning her attention to Dylan.

His wolf's eyes met hers and she knew his animal was right beneath the surface of his human skin. "Feels so good, Dylan." He sucked hard on her clit and she shuddered. "So good."

Good apparently wasn't enough for Dylan. No, because then he released her sex lips and two blunt fingertips teased her heat, the very center of her. 'Round and 'round he traced her opening, 'round and 'round increasing her arousal and adding to the pleasure coursing through her veins.

"Please…" She needed to be filled so, so badly. Stretched and filled and stroked until she came.

"We'll give you anything you want," Zeke's moist breath bathed her ear and then his rough cheek scraped hers. "Why don't you push those fingers inside her cunt, D? Give our mate what she needs."

The question barely left Zeke's mouth before Dylan did as directed. Those digits pressed deeply, sliding inside her sheath until he couldn't delve any farther.

She gasped with the fullness. Gasped and rocked against it, fucking herself on his hand. "Good. Fuck. So good." Lorelei once again tightened her hand in his hair, using him, taking what she needed from her mate. She couldn't wait to find out what it'd feel like to have them both possessing her. "Please."

Then it became a whirlwind of sensation. Dylan loved on her pussy, stroking, pumping, thrusting, and sucking. The movements sent more and more pleasure through her veins, her nerves reacting to each snippet of bliss that he gifted. Her moans and cries were echoed by Zeke's heavy breathing and Dylan's groans.

His ministrations remained constant, the regular rhythm sending her closer and closer to the edge until she knew her release was within reach.

It lurked on the edge of a cliff and she stretched for it, urging it to come closer and pushing her body nearer. She wanted to revel in the pleasure and bliss her mate caused.

Mate. Mate. Mate.

He'd be hers soon. They'd be hers soon.

"Oh, God. *Please*," she sobbed.

"Nibble on that clit, D." Zeke's voice was husky and deep. "Our girl likes a little pain."

And then Dylan did as Zeke asked, his hard fang skating over that bundle of nerves and then it was there. It was there within reach and she pounced, wrapping her arms around the bubble of pleasure.

She arched her back with the overwhelming release, the fire of her orgasm tearing through her veins and setting her nerves alight with the heat. It continued, the bliss enveloping her in a racing wind of joy. Her body trembled, muscles contracting and relaxing in a stuttering rhythm until she thought she'd die from the varying tempo.

Her pussy clenched and milked his fingers, and damn she wanted him inside her.

*Both* of them inside her. They would possess her at the same time and then sink their teeth into her flesh.

They'd claim her for their own.

And she couldn't wait.

*

Dylan slipped his fingers free of her weeping pussy, her heat clinging to him as if it didn't want to release his touch. He had to be honest, he didn't want to free her either.

But he did and the moment he left her warmth, he lifted his glistening fingers to his mouth. He held Lorelei's gaze as he slipped them between his lips and he sucked them clean, enjoying the salty sweet flavor of her cream. When he'd lapped up every drop, he released his treat and grinned at her.

"Delicious."

That drew a whimper from her and he knew she was half way to another release. Their mate was a sensual woman and he wanted to give her as much pleasure as possible.

She stroked his face, finger tracing the line of his jaw. "Thank you."

He grasped her wrist and turned her arm until her palm faced him. He placed a kiss to the center, following up the sweet move with a pinching nibble that drew another groan forward.

"My pleasure."

Her arousal swamped him, her continued desire for them fully evident.

But something else wrapped around him. Miles' and Holden's scents. His wolf howled in objection, demanding he wash her clean of them. Blood still marred the soft surface of her skin and he was quick to roll to his feet.

"Let's wash you and then we can see what else will make you scream." Dylan held out his hand to her, helping her from the counter while Zeke opened the shower door.

A handful of steps brought them all beneath the water. Several shower heads rained liquid on them, ensuring they were warmed by the sprays.

Zeke stepped after Lorelei, leaving her front facing him and bared to his gaze.

"Sweet, you're so beautiful. So ours." Dylan couldn't hold back the possessive words.

Lorelei simply trembled for him, her eyes glazing with desire.

"Let's get our mate clean and then we can move to other things." Zeke nuzzled her neck and Dylan took that as his cue to get to work.

He immediately reached for the soap dish. Tiny pre-wrapped soap rested on the small ledge along with—he picked up the small tube—waterproof lube. Quirking his brow, he showed it to Lorelei and Zeke.

"At least they're prepared." Lorelei grinned at him.

Dylan's knees went weak at the idea of preparation, at the concept of Zeke slicking his fingers and stretching their mate before taking possession.

"You shouldn't tease." He leaned over to set down the lube and snatch the soap, but a gentle hand on his arm had him turning back to her.

"Wherever you want, whenever you want, Dylan. I know you two won't hurt me and I," she licked her lips, "I want you just as much as you want me."

Zeke's wicked gaze met Dylan's, but his partner spoke into Lorelei's ear. "Talk like that is going to get you pressed between us, baby. It'll end up with one of us fucking your wet pussy while the other slides into your ass." His friend scraped a fang along her neck. "Has anyone been in your ass before? Do you like the burn?"

"I've never," she shook her head. "Never."

Dylan's cock hardened further at the admission and he was desperate to sink into her body, to claim her.

Instead of releasing the lube, he held it up and waved it slightly. "Who do you want in your virgin ass?"

He stepped closer, close enough that his cock brushed the softness of her stomach. He fought his release, demanded his damn cock hold back. Shooting before he got inside her, before he bit and claimed her, would mean starting over again. He needed to find his control.

Lorelei didn't say a word, but Zeke reached past her and snatched the tube. "I want to stretch her and push into her. Besides," he flashed his friend a grin. "You'd split her apart."

Dylan grimaced and prayed Lorelei didn't ask about Zeke's statement. Zeke and Dylan were partners, but they weren't sexual with each other. That didn't mean they didn't get a look at each other while sharing a woman. And more than once, a chick had complained about Dylan's girth.

Zeke was right. For the first time, his friend would claim her there.

"How… How do we do this?" Her voice was timid and soft, but his wolf-enhanced hearing allowed him to catch her words.

"Leave it to us." Dylan stepped even closer and leaned down, pressing his lips to hers. He delved into her mouth, tasting and hunting those flavors that made his wolf howl. She was so sensual and sweet and everything he'd ever dreamed of in a mate.

In the dark, when no one could read his thoughts, he'd often fantasized about finding a mate. At the time, it was thought that Wardens couldn't have a female of their own, but now… Now she was a reality.

He moaned against her lips, growling when a small warm hand encircled his cock. She stroked him, sliding over his length from root to tip. When she got to the head, she rubbed his slit before retracing her path. He sucked her tongue in time with the caress of his dick, teasing them both with the sensations.

When she gasped and trembled, he knew Zeke was toying with her ass, teasing the pucker and sinking a finger into her. It was always the same—pet, one finger, two, and then three to be followed by his cock.

The thoughts had Dylan's cock twitching in her hand.

Damn. Just, damn.

They continued that way, her touch edging him closer to release while her little moans and whimpers pushed him further. That didn't mean he'd stop. It merely meant he'd think of baseball. Which had him thinking of bases and the fact that he was about to hit a home run.

Baseball was a bad choice.

Thankfully Zeke saved him from coating Lorelei in his cum. "C'mon, baby. Wrap those legs around Dylan."

She was wrenched from his kiss, her hand abandoning him as well, but he didn't mind. Not when it meant seeing Zeke holding her for him, his hands gripping her thighs just above her knees and spreading those legs wide.

Wide for him.

"Wha—"

Dylan stepped forward, gaze centered on her exposed pussy. She glistened for him, her arousal blatantly evident. He stroked her clit and let his fingers venture farther south. "Do you want me here?" He pushed them deep. "Do you want me to fill your pussy while Zeke takes your ass? We're going to claim you, Lorelei.

We're going to fuck and bite you and then no one can take you from us." He kept his gaze serious, eyes boring into her. "And we'll kill anyone who tries."

Lorelei's eyes widened, but her nod was immediate.

"Then let's make you ours." He stepped toward the couple, one hand on his cock as he stroked himself, teasing before filling her. Once he got close, he gripped the base of his dick and pressed his cockhead to her entrance. With gentle, slow movements, he sank into her, pushing farther and farther until her pussy rested against him.

With Zeke still supporting her, he brushed a kiss over her lips. "You're mine."

"Yes," she hissed, wiggling her hips and rolling them with a sensuous glide.

"Let's allow Zeke to make you his, too."

"Yes," another hiss escaped her lips.

Dylan gently took Lorelei's weight, her curves easily embracing his body. She hugged his shoulders, nails digging into his skin and adding a sting of pain to the pleasure of being inside her.

"Oh, Dylan. Zeke's…" The words were a breathy whisper and then her deep moan told him that his partner breeched her back entrance.

The pressure around his cock increased, squeezing him tighter as his partner slid deeper into her body.

Lorelei sobbed, body trembling against him, but all he scented was pure need. She wanted them, craved them.

"We're gonna make you scream, sweet. You ready for that?" Dylan murmured.

She nodded. "Please…"

Without a word, they began their sexual dance. Zeke slid free of her heat and when he pressed forward, Dylan retreated. They filled her, alternating while giving all three of them pleasure.

His cock ached—still—but his canines also throbbed with a small pain as they slid free of his gums. His wolf howled and growled, yipping in anticipation of claiming her.

It wouldn't be long now. Already her pussy clutched him, milking him with each thrust and retreat. It was a tormenting rhythm that seemed to call for his release. He couldn't wait to give it to her.

The sound of their bodies meeting warred with the patter of rain on the tiles and the moans and groans that escaped their mouths.

Still, they continued, working harder, moving faster. His balls trembled and drew up tightly against his body, hardening, and he battled to keep his orgasm at bay.

*Not yet. Not yet.*

Soon, though. Very soon if Zeke's grunts and groans were anything to go by. After all these years, he knew his friend was close to the end of his rope.

They just needed Lorelei to join them.

"Are you going to come for us, sweet?" He grunted when she tightened on him, that squeeze harder than the last. "You gonna milk my cock while we fill you?" Another fist like tightening. "If you come for us, we'll give you everything. Come inside you, bite you, claim you."

The last few words came out as a growl, but he didn't care. Not when pleasure-glazed eyes met his and he knew his words had pushed her to the edge.

"Soon," she whispered.

Dylan's orgasm rested just out of sight as well, seeming to lurk within reach without rushing forward. God, he wanted to let go, wanted to make her his.

She would be his mate, their mate, but most of all… she'd be the beginning of his family. Not someone else's, not his brother's.

Zeke and Lorelei would be *his* future.

"Lorelei!" He snarled and that seemed to be all she needed.

The milking sped, her body trembled and a rough sob escaped her mouth.

With that, Dylan let himself go. He released the stranglehold he'd held on his orgasm and allowed it to run rampant through his body.

His cock pulsed and jerked, swelling inside her. When his partner shoved deep, the pressure increased, sending the pleasure attacking him sky high. He roared with his release, the bliss hammering him as his fangs fully descended. His mouth watered with the need to bite her.

Dylan met Zeke's gaze for a bare moment and he jerked his head in a nod. It was time. Without hesitating further, he lowered his head and did what he'd been dreaming of since he laid eyes on Lorelei.

He sank his teeth into her, sliding deeper and deeper with the sharp fangs. Her blood filled his veins, sending a new pulse of desire, and his body shuddered with the new pleasure.

His wolf danced and yipped with the claiming but that other part of him—his magic—did something else. It wove around them, his power mixing and mingling with Lorelei's until he couldn't sense where he ended and she began. It filled them, surrounded them and crept into every part of his body. He knew Zeke was experiencing something similar, his partner's feelings and experiences reaching Dylan without a thought.

Their magic was binding them all together.

The explosive light of their coming together overran the bathroom, blinding him until he was forced to close his eyes. But that didn't mean he stopped his attentions.

No, blood continued to flow, his cock continued to fill her and she was overcome with another release. They were a ball of pleasure, each shift and twitch of muscle spurring their bliss once again.

It took time, minutes ticking past, before Lorelei finally slumped between them and Dylan slowly slipped his fangs free of her flesh. He leaned back, still carefully cradling her body, and stared at his claiming mark. It was deep and purple, blood still sluggishly escaping, but it was *his* mark. *His.*

A glance to her opposite shoulder showed that Zeke had claimed her just as fully, ensuring that all others knew she belonged to a pair of powerful wolves.

He lapped at her wound, Zeke doing the same, until the flow of blood slowed and finally ceased. She was sated, exhausted, thoroughly loved and completely claimed.

All was right in Dylan's world. Years of being an outsider, of not truly belonging, were at an end. Dylan's future lay in his arms. Part of him didn't want to release her. No, he wanted to hold her close and never let her go.

Unfortunately, his cock softened, gently slipping from her sheath, and she moaned. When she whined, he figured Zeke had left her as well. Their poor mate was empty.

The moment she was cleaned—again—he would slide into her once more.

Zeke supported her as he slowly stepped back, allowing her feet to slip to the ground.

When she whined, he was quick to soothe her. "Shh... Let's wash you off and then we'll take you again, make you scream for us. You want that, sweet?"

Eyes closed, she gave him a slow, languorous nod.

Dylan quickly washed his mate, ridding her of the other wolves' scents. Before long, he was done and they all stepped from the shower. Lorelei was slowly coming around, her thoughts no longer muddled by pleasure and her eyes cleared of overwhelming arousal.

He couldn't wait to make her a victim to the pleasure once again.

Minutes later they were only damp and padding back into the bedroom. Lorelei was the first to crawl into bed.

And she actually crawled. On her hands and knees, ass tipped up and pussy exposed, she made her way across the mattress. Already his cock twitched and filled, anxious to sink into her again and again and again.

In the middle of the bed, she glanced over her shoulder with a wicked grin. The little tease knew exactly what she was doing. Smile still in place, she went back into motion, but before she settled completely, her attention was caught by... something on the floor near the door.

Dylan strode toward what'd obviously been slid under the door. He snatched the piece of paper and pen from the ground and flipped the page over.

*Please describe your claiming sex:*

*A) Amazing*

*B) Fantabulous*

*C) Squishy**

*D) All the Above*

**It is a family tradition that all women state their claiming sex is squishy. You don't want to go against family tradition, do you?*

Dylan chuckled and shook his head as he approached the bed. Zeke was now relaxed on the surface with Lorelei snuggled close.

"What's that?" Lorelei raised her eyebrows.

"A message from your cousins." Dylan smiled as he passed it over, the smile growing when his mate laughed.

She laid the page on the bed, made a large circle and then passed it back to him. "Far be it from me that I ruin family tradition."

Taking it from her grip, he went back to the door and bent down to slide both the paper and pen back into the hallway.

"Yes! Ha!" Scarlet's shout was unmistakable and Dylan rolled his eyes.

The rapid patter of her feet on the carpet announced her retreat, but he yelled after her anyway. "It's creepy to wait outside the door when someone inside is having sex!"

Dylan didn't get an answer, then again, he didn't wait for one. Not when he had a mate waiting for him.

A mate and a future. Life didn't get any better.

# Chapter Seven

Life just got worse.

Dylan crossed his arms over his chest and allowed his wolf to ease closer to the edge of his control. His magic was in rapid pursuit, unwilling to be left out of the confrontation. His skin crackled with the power and his eyes slowly slipped to their yellow hue.

Zeke and Lorelei were still tangled in the bed, sheets twisted around their entwined bodies. The scent of sex and blood still filled the air and that thought allowed a rush of desire to nudge forward. They'd made love, teased, tormented, and occasionally fucked, all night long. He'd tasted each inch of her body, reveling in her sweat and sweetness. When they'd decided they were too sticky to continue in bed, they'd moved back to the shower. Forty-five minutes and two rounds of love making later, they'd emerged into their room and found the mattress was covered in new linens.

Housekeeping was smart and didn't bother replacing the comforter.

Now, exhausted and sated, he had to face off against the Ruling Alphas *and* Ruling Wardens. When they'd said their trio would get one night, they hadn't been kidding.

"The answer is no." He shook his head. They had to be smoking crack if they thought he'd go along with their plan.

"You don't think—" Madden practically shouted, the physically stronger of the two Ruling Alphas wasn't used to being denied.

"Keep. Your voice. Down." Dylan remained in control and kept his words soft. Soft, but no less fierce. "You don't think Lorelei has been through enough? You don't think the three of us have dealt with enough? She submitted to the damned Wardens. We let those males *put their mouths* on our mate. They drank her blood and she had to use her magic to make them let go." Dylan stepped forward, pushing them farther into the hallway and from their shared room. "Why do you need Lorelei anyway? Miles and Holden took enough from her. What else do they need that they don't already have? What's it been? Eight? Ten hours? They still haven't found her? Are they even trying?"

Dylan had nearly lost control when Lorelei told them of the Wardens' actions. They weren't going to let go. They'd craved every bit of her blood and would have drained her had she not protected herself. The minute Paisley was found, he would have a meeting of the magics with those two.

Levy sighed. "It's not that simple. She's not in the hotel and while Hotel Garou is isolated, ten miles down the road we've got a big city. They're still going block by block and expanding their search areas as much as they can. We want to draw some of the wolves out. Give them the opportunity to get at Lorelei."

Emmett grimaced. "Look, I know she's your mate and if it was me, I'd kick your ass for this suggestion, but we don't have any other options."

Dylan rubbed his forehead, considering their request. Hell, order really.

Leave Lorelei alone in their suite. Alone with monitoring devices so Emmett and Levy could go in at a moment's notice, but by herself none the less.

His Lorelei. Their Lorelei.

He'd grown up knowing he'd never have a mate, that he and Zeke would only ever have each other. And… he'd been fine with that. *Fine.*

But then there was Whitney, Emmett, and Levy…

Hope blossomed in his chest, an emotion he'd kept close. He didn't let even Zeke ferret out his feelings.

Hope for a family of his own.

The Ruling Alphas and Wardens wanted him to risk that.

He didn't deny it was for a good cause, but Lorelei was their *mate*. Hadn't he lost enough?

It wasn't like he loved her, but… He couldn't love her, right? It was too soon for that. But that didn't mean when he looked at her¬—when he watched her ride him, nibble her lower lip, and then sob his name—he didn't feel the stirrings of the emotion. Yes, it trembled in his chest, pleading to be set free and he knew Zeke experienced the same sensations. They didn't love her, but God how they wanted to.

Emmett, Levy, Keller, and Madden's plan threatened that dream. Threatened to batter, bruise, and destroy any hope for happiness he'd had for the last year.

"Think of Paisley, Dylan." Keller's words were low and pleading. "She's as good as your sister now. Do you want her to suffer under his hand? Because if they don't have her yet, I don't think it'll be long before they capture her."

"You're not playing fair." He heaved in a breath and let it out slowly.

"There is no fair when it comes to these wolves. You know that." Madden was grim. "If there was, Maxim wouldn't be pulling this shit. He gave his vow to Keller and me that there'd be no repercussions after last year's battle. That he held no ill will and the family was a friend of the Ruling Alphas."

No, there wasn't fair when it came to his older brother. There never had been. He was just like their father in that respect.

"I—" His wolf snarled, sensing Dylan's wavering conviction. Because Paisley was as good as his sister.

The men before him were as good as blood cousins. They were all tied together by the Wickham and Twynham women and the family needed them. No, they needed Lorelei.

"What makes you think he'll go after Lorelei? She's already mated to me and Zeke. There's no undoing that. Why do you think my brother will still want her?" That was one thing Dylan didn't understand. "They want revenge on the Wickhams because of Whitney's actions last year. So, they're settling for the Twynham sisters, and the male who attacked Rebecca specifically said their goal was to keep more Wickham—Twynham—blood out of the wolves."

Every male's face turned grim, some closing their eyes to shut him out and others avoiding his gaze entirely.

Seconds passed and Dylan's wolf became more and more agitated with each fleeting moment. Something wasn't being said. "What?"

Levy finally responded. "We'll…" The Warden sighed. "We will suppress your mating." He was quick to rush out the rest. "We won't break it, but we can muffle it enough to make her scent like an unmated female."

"You want to…" No. *No.* He stumbled back until he collided with the hallway wall. His heart clenched and froze until he thought he'd die from the pain. His wolf howled in objection while his magic crackled and stung his skin.

To suppress…

"It's temporary, Dylan. No more than a day. If they don't take the bait, we'll come up with another idea." Emmett picked up where Levy left off. "The men surrounding Maxim are mostly idiots. We doubt it'll take long for one of them to make a try for them. Hopefully two will appear."

"Them? Make a try for them?" Which one of the males was stupid enough to let their mate be bait? He shook his head. He knew who. The only other Twynham in residence. "What'd you do to Aidan and Carson to convince them to let this happen? And if you already have Rebecca, why do you need Lorelei?"

Dylan would do whatever he could to keep Lorelei out of harm's way.

"Two is better than one, Dylan," Keller tried again.

Dylan let his head drop back, eyes trained on the ceiling. "You guys don't understand."

"We know that no wolf wants to lose his mate, Dylan. We'll do everything we can to keep her safe." Emmett was quick to reassure him. Too bad it didn't.

"No. You really don't understand." He focused on Levy. "She is everything, Levy. You saw some of my past, you know why every second with her is…"

Just everything. She didn't love him yet, he knew that, but what she did feel filled in the dark gaps and cracks in his heart. Zeke's family had tried their hardest to break him over the years, but Lorelei took her healing beyond that pain. She didn't just soothe his wolf, she rubbed off the rough edges of his shattered soul.

No one could understand that. No one. To lose her…

"I understand, Dylan." Levy whispered the words. "I know and it kills me to come to you like this, but we don't have a choice. It's taking Miles and Holden too long. Even with Lorelei's blood," he shook his head, "it's not enough."

"I'll do it." The lyrical voice was a little hoarse, her screams and sobs from last night stealing the smoothness.

Dylan pushed away from the wall and turned to face his mate. She was wrapped in the blanket that'd covered the bed, not a hint of her body visible to the men. That wasn't enough for the wolf though. No, the fact that she was naked beneath the fabric had the beast snarling. Where the hell was Zeke? He should have kept her hidden inside or at least forced her to put clothes on. Then he heard a very familiar snore. Damn man slept like the dead.

"Lorelei…" He took a step toward her and he nearly crumbled beneath her pleading gaze.

"I have to, Dylan. I *have to.*"

He swallowed through the emotion clogging his throat, fighting for breath to speak. "Lorelei, I can't lose you. I *can't.*"

She didn't understand. No one did. Not even Levy, really.

Lorelei came to him and leaned against him, resting her head on his chest. "I know."

"No, you…"

"Yes." She propped her chin on his chest, over his heart. "You're not the only one who can share thoughts, Dylan. Or take a peek." He flinched but she kept speaking. "I don't know how to control it, but I saw. So, I understand. But you also know why I have to do this, don't you?"

Dylan closed his eyes, shutting out the beautiful vision before him. Yes, he did know. The connection between the three sisters was tight and unbreakable. They'd leaned on each other, taking comfort, and supported each other through every trial. But truly, it all went back to when Rebecca was hurt. They'd formed a bond during those months of the woman's recovery and now they would do anything to keep the other safe.

"I know," he whispered and then focused on Emmett. "What has to happen?"

Levy answered, "We'll suppress their matings and put them in your hotel room. The rogues already know where Rebecca's room is and they know we'll be on guard for an attack there. Instead, both women will be in yours." Levy's gaze shifted from Dylan to Lorelei and back again. "We'll be in the suite directly above. It'll take a single thought to drop through the floor and capture whoever attacks."

"And what if it's Maxim? What then? He has the Grimoire. Either ours or Sarvis', remember? He'll be powerful." Dylan had no doubt about that fact.

The Ruling Alphas shook their heads. "No, he's smarter than to come himself. He'll send disposables to try and get them. He'll stay in hiding and expect them to bring the women to him. He won't make himself that vulnerable."

"You know it has to happen, D." Zeke's hand came to rest on his shoulder, giving him a gentle squeeze. Their discussion had obviously awakened his partner.

"I'm outnumbered." He gave a sad chuckle. "It doesn't really matter then, does it?"

"Can you guys give us a minute?" Lorelei formed it as a question, but the order was unmistakable and their visitors padded back the way they came. The moment they were out of sight, she forced him to stare into her eyes. "It will always matter. What you two feel will *always* matter. Any other time, any other situation, and we'd all come to some sort of agreement. But Dylan, this is my sister. She…"

Dylan cupped her cheek, recognizing that his delay merely upset her more. "I know. I just don't wanna lose you. This has to happen and I support you. I needed to get my fears on the table. I can't lose you, *we* can't lose you, Lorelei. Not when we just found you."

"I won't go anywhere." Her eyes filled with tears and when one snaked down her cheek, he brushed it away with his thumb. "I have something really, really good to come back to."

Dylan leaned down and pressed his lips to the top of her head, closing his eyes against the moisture gathering behind his lids. "I won't tell you that I love you, Lorelei. I will say that if something happened to you, if they managed to hurt you, my heart would die alongside yours. It's not worth beating if you're not with me."

Zeke's heat enveloped them and he knew his partner eased closer, bracketing Lorelei with their bodies. "It'd destroy us, Lorelei. If the worst happened and they got their hands on you… No matter what, you've gotta live. Live and we'll find you."

They would come for her and kill anyone who stood in the way.

It wasn't a half-hearted promise, it was a soul binding vow.

* * *

The waiting would kill Lorelei. Every slam of a door down the hall had her jumping, and each time the AC kicked on, she trembled.

It didn't help that she felt as if ants crawled over her skin, biting and pinching her flesh. It hurt, but it didn't. It was hot, but it was cold. When she glanced at Rebecca, she found her sister was in the same shape.

She rubbed her arms, fighting to brush off the awkward sensations. The initial spell to blunt the connection to their mates hadn't been painful. It was simply a throbbing ache that enveloped her, pulsing in time with her heart. The journey to the suite hadn't been difficult, either. A couple of guards, a voiced promise to remain inside and that they'd send a wolf along to watch the door soon.

*Just don't open the door.*

Since that'd been Rebecca's downfall, the Ruling Alphas and Wardens hoped the men working with Maxim were dumb enough to fall for the blatant trap.

As they'd said, the first guy was beyond an idiot.

Rebecca twitched. Another tremble wracked her youngest sister.

Hadn't she suffered enough for the damned wolves? For all of… this bullshit?

Lorelei crossed to her sister and lowered to the couch, wrapping an arm around her shoulders the moment she was settled. "Hey, you okay?"

Rebecca chuckled. "Not even close."

"Yeah," she sighed, "I know."

"It's like the burns are back and fresh. Eating away at me." Her sister's voice was hoarse and strained.

"It'll be okay. I made them promise that if nothing happens in the first twelve hours, we're done."

"You can't put a timeline on idiots, Lor."

"Yeah, well, I can put a timeline on our suffering." She didn't think she could stand more than twelve hours of this. And if Rebecca was reliving the pain from the fire…

"You're happy, right, Lor?"

"Yeah." Lorelei leaned into Rebecca. "When I'm not feeling like I'm being eaten alive, I'm really happy. They're…"

Amazing. Frustrating. Gorgeous. Heart melting.

Hers.

"Yeah, mine too," Rebecca whispered. "Do you think, when we get Paisley back, she'll have mates, too?"

"I hope so." Lorelei couldn't think of anything better than having mates. Even if they were wolves and came in sets of two. And with magic. She couldn't forget that part.

Which had *her* power pulsing and nudging her. Dammit.

That was one thing they'd told her she absolutely could not use. The moment she let it rush forward and began glowing like the ball that drops on New Year's, they'd know she'd been mated. Or at least met her mates. She was too strong to have been merely an activated Warden Born.

That'd make this whole charade useless and the wolf—or wolves—could possibly get away.

So, Lorelei tamped it down, quietly begging that part of her to retreat for Paisley's sake. Slowly the energy receded, easing into the back of her mind and crawling deep into her body.

Lorelei pushed to her feet. "We can't just sit here and wait. Snag the remote and I'll raid the minibar. There's gotta be something worth snacking on."

"Don't you think we should remain, you know, vigilant?" Rebecca sounded unsure, but Lorelei was sticking to her plan.

"We can vigilantly eat chocolate covered raisins and keep the TV low. I just can't sit here waiting for the door to blow in."

And… that's when the door blew in.

Nice.

At least the idiots finally got their shit together.

Wood scattered, and the crack and thud of the panel being torn from the wall warred with her sister's surprised scream.

Three men strode through the entrance, their bodies perverted imitations of humans. Their faces were half wolf while their hands and arms were heavily muscled and coated with fur. Their fingers and hands were replaced by paws and claws, the men seeming more than ready to tear them into pieces.

Rebecca rose from the couch in a quick rush and Lorelei was just as fast to place herself between the intruders and her sister. Rebecca was scarred enough due to werewolves. She wasn't going to risk her sister being hurt further.

They had to go through her.

The males fanned out, one remaining in front of her while the other two tried to block her sides. Yeah, no. Not happening.

Lorelei eased backwards, nudging Rebecca along. Getting to the door wasn't gonna happen, but all she needed to do was hold the men off until the cavalry showed up.

Like, any time now. They supposedly set up some sort of spell. If anyone entered—anyone—Emmett and Levy would be notified. Then they'd haul Lorelei and Rebecca's mates into the suite as well as the Ruling Alphas. Lotsa testosterone in an instant.

Instead, they were still alone.

"Where are they?" Rebecca whispered, but she knew the supposed leader heard.

An evil grin filled his features. "Your little friends don't know we're here. Blood magic has its benefits." The man raised a hand and she noticed splashes of burgundy marring his skin. "Something your Ruling

Wardens aren't willing to accept. Know what else?" That grin turned into a feral smile. "They didn't use your blood for this lovely little spell and only focused on your family." He chuckled. "Blood from your family gets past the barrier without a problem."

Lorelei bent at the waist, clutching at her stomach as she realized… the deep hue wasn't paint. It was… "Paisley."

"She's very pretty. Much like you two. And I can definitely see the family resemblance to the Wickhams." He clucked his tongue and shook his head. "Too bad we can't get those three, but they've already tainted the wolves. We'll settle for stopping their cousins."

"She's alive?" The two men at Lorelei's sides eased closer.

"For now," the man on her left sneered.

"Can't make promises." The man on her right chuckled. "She's a pretty one. Who knows what Ma—"

"*Enough*," their leader snarled. "Get them and let's go. The magic got us in here, but it can't hide us from prying eyes. We need to leave before anyone sees that door."

"But, see, here's the thing." Lorelei licked her lips and straightened fully. She let her arms hang loose at her sides, relaxed but ready for whatever they had. "That's not gonna happen."

"We're at the wall," Rebecca whispered.

“You’re gonna stay really still. ’Kay? I’ll take care of this.” Lorelei didn’t let a hint of unease or nervousness enter her voice. She’d trained-ish for this, right? Albeit she hadn’t planned on more than one attacker, but she could do this.

She hoped.

If what the man said was true, these three got in undetected so she needed to keep her and Rebecca safe while making as much noise as possible. The damned wolves had good hearing, right?

“Take care of this?” The main guy snorted. “Just give in and maybe you’ll live through this, huh? We can neutralize you and send you three on your way.”

Neutralize…

“What do you mean?” It’d be great if the asshole revealed his plan.

Like, super great.

“Enough.” He flicked his gaze to the other two men. “Take her. Quietly.”

The only thing that saved her, at least at first, was the fact they came one at a time.

The first guy—Asshole One—raced forward, hands outstretched and not even attempting to protect his body. Well, sucked to be him. He’d probably been banking on her being inexperienced like Paisley and Rebecca. Let him think that. At least until she broke a bone or two. Not that she had in the past. Hitting a bag and kicking a man in the knee were two different things.

But that difference didn't have him stopping. No, he vaulted over the couch and shoved one of the end tables aside. He wasn't schooled in fighting and was probably used to depending on bulk and strength to get by.

The second he was within range, she went after him. She didn't hesitate. Hell, she didn't think. No, she just… let it all go.

She'd been attacked once. It was the reason for the gun and the self-defense lessons. A woman was motivated to protect herself when she'd experienced violence. She would never have another black eye or split lip. A gun would never again be pressed against her forehead and she wouldn't cower before a male with tears in her eyes. Ever.

She punched him in the eye with a quick jab and followed it with a cross to his cheek. Then came a hook to his jaw and a nice uppercut to his chin.

Asshole One didn't go down, but he was dazed and despite the throbbing of her fist, she was damned proud of herself. He shook his head and straightened, taking another step toward them. Well, what'd she expect? A big guy like that—a werewolf—wouldn't be disabled.

When he stepped forward this time, she shifted her position and went for the knee, kicking it on the side and enjoying the nice crunch that came with the move. He toppled to the ground, clutching his injury. Now on his knees, it made it easy for her to kick him again, this one right to his face, left to right and in the perfect spot to… Send him tumbling to the floor unconscious.

One down, two to go and she doubted those tactics would work a second time.

"*No!*" Lorelei knew that scream and she cursed herself for not watching after Rebecca.

Asshole Two got his hands on her. He wrapped his arm around her neck, forearm pressed against her throat and her face slowly reddened. He was strangling her and she could do… nothing about it.

Her magic twitched and pulsed, reminding her it was still present. It was there, but who was she facing? Would she manage to get Rebecca free only to have the main guy take them both out before they found out where to find Paisley?

She split her attention between Rebecca and the male near the door. Her power pushed at its bindings and Lorelei let it free. Something inside her said to trust the magic, that it knew how best to deal with the situation. She was the conduit at this point, unable to direct the sizzling magic.

Lorelei watched it dart forward, skim the main male and then Asshole Two, flicking them with an invisible tendril before telling her the two wolves definitely weren't Wardens. Regular wolves. Weak. Oh, werewolves were physically superior to both Rebecca and Lorelei, but she had something they didn't.

"Let her go." She kept her tone smooth. The last thing she wanted to do was alert them of what was to come. The crackle of her rising power teased her skin, but she fought to keep the telltale glow under wraps. She had to surprise Asshole Two.

Asshole Two snorted. "Right. Because you said so?"

"Look, just come with us," the man by the door said.

Now Lorelei snorted. "So you can kill us all? No."

"You either come along and have a chance at living or I can guarantee your sister will die. Now." The wolf by the door kept the words flat and emotionless.

Lorelei glanced at Rebecca and the purple hue that showed her sister was nearing the end of her oxygen-infused rope.

"Last chance." She tilted her head toward her sister. "Let her go." When he shook his head, she mirrored the move. "I gave you fair warning, huh? Remember that."

Lorelei released it, let the gathering magic free into the air to do as it wished. The glaring glow of her skin hurt her eyes, but she kept them open, soon becoming accustomed to the brightness. Then she watched. She watched and gestured and formed the power as she desired.

The tendrils didn't creep—they raced. They shot through the air and headed for the two offensive males. The one holding Rebecca was quickly subdued, a burn marring his skin while the energy stole his breath.

Apparently her magic was very eye-for-an-eye.

She attempted to communicate with that part of her. It was separate but the same, and the attacker couldn't be killed. At least, not yet. She had the impression it pouted.

Next she went after the fleeing male, reaching for him with those glowing, snaking coils. One wrapped around an ankle while another snared his wrist. It tugged and yanked, drawing him back into the suite. He sought escape, but her magic wouldn't let that happen.

It knew, just as Lorelei did, they were needed alive. More the pity.

So, she tugged, fought, and wrenched. Another twirling glow grabbed him and hauled him deeper into the room. She wouldn't let him flee. There was no way he'd take off without telling them everything he knew. There was no way…

He had a gun in his hand. His free hand. She'd left it untethered and he had a gun pointed at Rebecca and…

And Lorelei didn't think, didn't breathe, didn't even blink. No, her entire consciousness was focused on that weapon, at the flare of light and pop as it fired.

She didn't know how it happened, didn't know where the energy came from or how she wielded it, but she curled in on herself, air heaving from her lungs as she bent over. And as she rose, as she drew oxygen back into herself… she simply let go.

The light didn't come in gradual increments. Her power exploded. It overruled everything, every law of nature and man, and it filled every nook and cranny in the room. Hell, she had the feeling it moved beyond their small space. It sent Rebecca staggering and the main guy tripping backwards, but most importantly, it froze the bullet in place. It immobilized it midair, keeping it suspended.

It saved Rebecca. Saved her and she was uninjured and the magic could recede now, but it wouldn't let go. It wouldn't quit hunting for a target, wouldn't stop trying to find someone else who threatened her and Rebecca. She begged the magic to return, to climb back into Lorelei before they hurt someone, before they destroyed an innocent…

"Lorelei!" She recognized that voice.

"Dammit, Lorelei!" Knew that one, too.

They were both safe, comforting. They were home.

The power would protect her home as well.

It wrapped around the men, drawing them closer as she tugged Rebecca nearer in their wake.

"Lorelei, you need to calm down." Dylan? Yes, Dylan urged her to calm. Why? She was fine.

"Pull it back, baby. It's out of control." If the first male was Dylan then this was Zeke. Sweet smiles and damned sexy.

If she pulled it back, they'd be vulnerable. No, she would not. They would discover she was right.

"Lor, you gotta stop." A soft, delicate hand landed on her shoulder. It was small and smooth, not rough and large like her mates. "We can't find Paisley this way."

Paisley. Yes. Paisley.

Lorelei reached for the writhing glow, the physical part of her that lived in the power, and drew it to her. She breathed deeply and exhaled slowly, fighting and clawing it back to her body. It battled her. It didn't want to be contained, but they needed the unconscious men to find Paisley. No one could help do that if they couldn't come near her. She had no doubt the magic would tear into anyone who wasn't theirs.

Rebecca was theirs

Zeke was theirs.

Dylan was theirs.

The glow slowly diminished, lessening with every beat of her heart. It dimmed the harder she tugged until her skin was a pale imitation of her natural color. Her twining Marks remained a pulsing reminder of her power, but at least it was banked.

For now.

God help the men who stole Paisley.

Calm and exhausted, she slumped into the men on her right, letting them take her weight, and she knew one of her mates swung her into his arms. She buried her face against his neck, inhaling his scent, allowing her to calm further.

"Check on Rebecca," she mumbled.

"Zeke has Rebecca. He'll get her to a Warden and her mates just as I'll get you to help." Dylan's voice rumbled through her, vibrating her from within.

"Don't let them get away."

Zeke chuckled. "Baby, we'll be lucky to wake them up."

"I can bring them back after my nap." She didn't know how she could, but there was no question in her mind.

"Okay, sweet. We might take you up on that." Dylan's lips brushed her forehead and she nuzzled him again.

"Was scared," she whispered.

"I know, we were, too. We didn't realize you were in trouble until you…" Zeke didn't finish his sentence.

"Exploded." The word was a grumble.

"How'd they get in?" The new voice, familiar and male, singed her nerves.

Her magic immediately reacted, coiling and tensing in preparation of attack. Dammit. She couldn't go after every man who came near.

Then a cool balm stroked her, the first joined by a second and she released a relieved sigh. Her mates. They were there, ready to smooth her still-ragged edges.

"Paisley," she licked her lips, hating the truth. "They used her blood. The spell was tied to our family line, not us individually." She peeked over Dylan's shoulder and noted the three unconscious men. "Their hands are painted red." A shudder wracked her. "It's her blood, but they talked about her as if she's still alive."

She turned back to the man. Levy. Levy and behind him was Emmett and they were Whitney's mates. Even farther were Keller and Madden with their mate Scarlet. *My cousin.*

Thoughts, memories, were slowly coming back. The longer she remained calm, the more that filtered through.

Carson and Aidan were there for Rebecca and Gabriella was there with Berke and Jack.

Her family.

"She is alive, Lor." Rebecca spoke with firm conviction and she prayed her youngest sister was right.

Because if they lost Paisley, she wasn't sure what she'd do. Hell, she wasn't sure what her *magic* would do.

Carson and Aidan twitched, bodies jerking, and she noted the gray covering their cheeks, the sharpness of their faces.

"Let them through." She cleared her throat and fought to speak louder. "Let Carson and Aidan through."

"You won't…" Levy raised his eyebrows and she recognized what they'd done.

Most Powerful Wardens first.

Most Dominant Alphas next.

Then Fierce Alphas.

And finally, the newest additions to the family.

They knew she wouldn't harm Rebecca or her own mates.

They weren't sure about anyone else.

"I promise. Let them come forward. Let them see for themselves that she's fine." Lorelei nodded.

Everyone slowly relaxed and then Rebecca's mates were there, hands stroking her body and growls filling the air when they spotted her neck.

Then it became a battle to keep Rebecca's mates from killing the prone men.

Slowly their group dispersed, everyone stepping into their roles, organizing clean up and securing the interlopers.

It happened around their trio, the activity manic while the three of them seemed to exist in a bubble. Dylan carried her to one of the untouched bedrooms and lowered to a cushioned chair, cradling her in his arms. Zeke tugged another close until she was warm and safe between them.

Safe.

She was safe.

"Are you okay, sweet? That was… amazing." Dylan didn't add that it was scary as hell, too.

"Baby?" Zeke echoed Dylan.

"I'm…" She took stock of herself, noting the aches and pains, but she was alive. Alive and safe and it was more than her sister had, wasn't it? "I'm okay. I'm…" She reached for Zeke and Dylan, clutching their hands. "I thought Rebecca was gonna die. I thought they'd kill her and you guys weren't there and then I—" She couldn't stop the sob that rose to her throat. One made way for two and she couldn't breathe through the crying. "I could have killed you. I could have killed them. It wanted to. I wanted to destroy them."

Both men squeezed her hands and it was Zeke who spoke first. "But you didn't. And I know how hard it is. When Dylan showed up on my doorstep all those years ago," Zeke brushed a strand of hair from her face and tucked it behind her ear, "he was battered, bloody, and bruised and I wanted to go after the man who'd done that to him. I wanted to bathe in the male's blood. Thirteen and more than anything, I wanted to destroy him." Lorelei let her gaze skitter away, but he wouldn't let it. "Wanting to hurt someone who hurt a loved one is nothing to be ashamed of. Everyone has rage. True, you're a little more dangerous than most, but just because you can end someone's life doesn't mean you will."

"I almost did," she whispered, hating herself for her actions. "I'm as evil as they are. As twisted and broken and—"

"But you didn't and that's what matters." Zeke cupped her cheeks and his gaze grew intent and serious. "The woman we mated, the woman who will bear our cubs, and the woman we love is not evil. She's so full of goodness and caring that she was willing to risk her life. Those aren't the actions of an evil person."

Tears burned her eyes and she fought to blink them back. "You," she sniffled, "you love me?"

Did he? Was he just telling her what she needed to hear?

"You know I do and if you look in Dylan's heart, you'll see he does, too."

Lorelei tipped her head back and met Dylan's gaze. "Is that true?"

"Only if you want it to be. The last thing we want to do is scare you." Dylan traced her lips with a finger. "A mating starts with a wolf's instincts and nature's guidance, but our hearts are our own. How could we not love a woman who risked so much for someone she loves? We just hope you return our feelings someday."

"I already do." The words were low, but when their eyes blazed yellow and a dusting of gray hair invaded their cheeks, she knew they'd heard her.

Yes, she already did love them—there was no question—and she hoped to love them for a very long time.

Hopefully as long as Paisley would love her mates. Once they found her and she found them. Because, above all, she *knew* her sister would be found. Found. And someday Paisley would discover the happiness she shared with Zeke and Dylan.

They just might have to kill a few people along the way.

# THE END

If you enjoyed this book, please be totally awesomesauce and leave a review so others may discover it as well. Long review or short, your opinion will help other readers make future purchasing decisions. So, go forth and rate my level-o-awesome!

By the way… you can check at the rest of the Alpha Marked series on Celia's website: http://celiakyle.com/alphamarked

# About Celia Kyle

Ex-dance teacher, former accountant and erstwhile collectible doll salesperson, New York Times and USA Today bestselling author Celia Kyle now writes paranormal romances for readers who:

1) Like super hunky heroes (they generally get furry)
2) Dig beautiful women (who have a few more curves than the average lady)
3) Love laughing in (and out of) bed.

It goes without saying that there's always a happily-ever-after for her characters, even if there are a few road bumps along the way.

Today she lives in Central Florida and writes full-time with the support of her loving husband and two finicky cats.

If you'd like to be notified of new releases, special sales, and get FREE eBooks, subscribe here: http://celiakyle.com/news

You can find Celia online at:

http://celiakyle.com
http://facebook.com/authorceliakyle
http://twitter.com/celiakyle

# Copyright Page

Made in the USA
Lexington, KY
22 February 2015